"Don't be mad at me," Jace said softly.

His voice was like cool silk on her raw feelings, but Rebecca didn't welcome the sensation.

"I'm not mad at you," she said, remembering not to trust him. "I told you before, I don't feel anything for you."

Jace seized her hand. "And I told you before, I don't believe you."

"What do I have to do to make you believe me, so you'll leave me alone?" she asked.

"Kiss me." The words rang with challenge, and beneath the challenge ran smoky desire. "Kiss me and tell me you don't feel anything, Becca."

What choice did she have? She didn't want Jace in her life. This was the perfect chance to prove that to him. Ignoring the sense of impending doom that weighed on her, Rebecca sank to the bed beside him. Jace wove his fingers through her hair and angled her head as he lowered his.

At the first brush of his lips across hers, she was lost. Sensation and memories twined like silken ribbons around her, binding her to a deep truth—no man had ever made her feel the way Jace did. . . .

WHAT ARE *LOVESWEPT* ROMANCES?

They are stories of true romance and touching emotion. We believe those two very important ingredients are constants in our highly sensual and very believable stories in the *LOVESWEPT* line. Our goal is to give you, the reader, stories of consistently high quality that may sometimes make you laugh, sometimes make you cry, but are always fresh and creative and contain many delightful surprises within their pages.

Most romance fans read an enormous number of books. Those they truly love, they keep. Others may be traded with friends and soon forgotten. We hope that each *LOVESWEPT* romance will be a treasure—a "keeper." We will always try to publish

LOVE STORIES YOU'LL NEVER FORGET
BY AUTHORS YOU'LL ALWAYS REMEMBER

The Editors

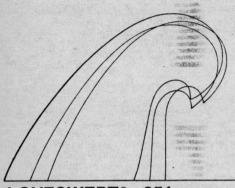

LOVESWEPT® • 351

Tami Hoag
Straight from the
Heart

BANTAM BOOKS
NEW YORK • TORONTO • LONDON • SYDNEY • AUCKLAND

One

"Jace Cooper's coming back to town!"

Rebecca Bradshaw's hand slipped on the edge of the whirlpool, and she dropped her clipboard into the churning water. Water splashed up onto the newspaper her patient, Bob Wilkes, held open just above the surface and sprayed onto the front of her white smock.

"Hey!" Yanking his paper out of the way, Bob gave her an indignant look. "Jeez, Rebecca, what if that had been a radio or a hair dryer or something?"

She frowned, more at her reaction to the news about Jace Cooper that Bob had read aloud than at him. "You would have gotten a free hairdo. May I have my board back, please?"

Bob's wide mouth lifted in the comic leer he had used on her on a regular basis over the last few months of his physical therapy. "Why don't you come and get it, beautiful?"

Rebecca slanted him a look. "Fork it over, Romeo, or I'll put you back on the tilt table and spin that thing like a roulette wheel."

Wilkes handed her the dripping clipboard with its sheaf of soggy papers. "You're heartless, a sadist."

"Flattery will get you nowhere," she said. As she tried to blot her notes and her sweater with a towel, unbidden thoughts of Jace Cooper tormented her. She quelled the urge she had to pump Bob for more information.

But as if he'd read her mind, he went on. "It says here that Cooper's being sent down to the Mavericks. He'll be playing here in Mishawaka if he can get his knee back in shape." Wilkes shook his head. "How do you like that? The guy gives the Chicago Kings six and a half great seasons. He's been an All-Star, he's been a Golden Glove winner. Now he gets wracked up, and they pack him off to the minors without so much as a fond farewell. He goes from the big show back to Class A ball overnight. That stinks."

"I imagine they got sick of his shenanigans off the field," Dominique LeGault said as she worked with a patient on the mat table.

Rebecca glanced up at her coworker. Dominique was a woman of rare and exotic beauty. She was a long-limbed six footer, with skin the color of *café au lait* and almond-shaped eyes that reflected her mother's Cherokee heritage.

Dominique shook her head, her wild cloud of black hair bouncing behind her. "With all his partying, practical jokes, and publicity stunts, that man was in and out of more trouble than the rest of his team put together."

"What a guy does on his time is his own business," Wilkes declared. "Which reminds me, Rebecca, do you want to watch a movie with me tonight?" He chuckled mischievously. "*Bimbos Galore* is now available on videocassette."

"As much as I've been waiting for that, I'll have to

pass," she said firmly. "You know I don't date patients, Bob."

"Bad policy," he muttered.

It was a policy Rebecca had adhered to strictly during her nine years as a physical therapist. The one exception she had made to that rule—Jace Cooper—had turned out to be the biggest mistake of her life.

She pushed the thought from her mind as she abandoned her ruined notes and went to a cabinet against the far wall of the exercise room to get out the toolbox and the coffee can of miscellaneous screws, nuts, bolts, and pins. She had a patient with a spinal cord injury coming in an hour to make her first attempt at using the parallel bars, and the bars had to be adjusted.

Rebecca told herself she had no time to reflect on the news that Jace Cooper was coming back to town. What did she care? She didn't. The news had just surprised her, that was all.

"Jace Cooper," Mrs. Krumhansle, Dominique's patient, mused aloud. She scratched a hand back through her steel gray hair. "Isn't he the cute one with the ash blond hair and the great fanny?"

Dominique's hoarse laugh filled the air. "That's him."

"Good glove. Swings a mean bat when he wants to. I'll have to renew my season ticket."

"It seems to me we're doing a lot more talking than working in here today," Rebecca said sharply.

Bob Wilkes gave a low whistle and hid behind his newspaper. Dominique's exotic black eyes focused on Rebecca's from across the room. Rebecca dodged the question in her friend's gaze.

Concentrating on the task at hand, she squatted down and began to work on the piece of therapy equipment. She certainly had better things to think of than some overage adolescent getting kicked off his team.

She had her next patient to think of. She had the proposed expansion of the physical therapy department to think of. She wondered if there was any way she was going to be able to talk the hospital board into providing a separate hydrotherapy room. She wondered what Jace Cooper had done to his knee.

"No, no, Rebecca," she muttered under her breath, shaking her head so her glossy black hair swung back and forth above her shoulders.

It upset her that the mere mention of the man could throw her into such a mental tailspin. Jace Cooper had ceased to be a part of her life. She had accepted that fact, had dealt with it. It wasn't as if she'd been carrying a torch for him. She'd dated other men over the years, had enjoyed other relationships. Jace Cooper didn't mean anything to her. He didn't matter a whit, not one iota.

Not more than ten feet away from her, the door to the therapy room was pushed open by Dr. Cornish. Rebecca's gaze landed on the man resting on crutches beside the doctor.

He had the lean, tough good looks of an alley cat who'd won more fights than he'd lost. His hair was a little shaggy, dark at the roots but gradually lightening to a distinctive silver blond at the ends. Navy blue eyes stared at her from beneath dark brows.

As her heart went into a frenzied dance, Rebecca bolted to her feet, hitting her head on the bar. She dropped her screwdriver and upended the coffee can. Hardware spilled onto the smooth floor. Nuts and washers skittered off in all directions.

A tiny smile lifted one corner of Jace Cooper's mouth. "Well, Becca," he said softly, "you never were the mechanical one in your family."

•   •   •

"No." Rebecca's eyes burned with an emerald fire as she stared at Dr. Donald Cornish.

At five feet ten inches, she had no need to lift her head to look the balding, middle-aged doctor in the eye. She wasn't intimidated either by his disgruntled expression or by the tag on his white jacket that identified him as head of orthopedics.

Even though Rebecca was only thirty, she was the boss in physical therapy and everyone at the hospital knew it. Besides, she thought as she glanced out the window of her office at the man who was holding court in the exercise room, she would have stared down the devil himself to get out of working with Jace Cooper.

She watched as he grinned and laughed at something Bob Wilkes said. Jace had the kind of charm that attracted people to him. Everyone automatically liked him. He was charismatic. He was dangerous.

A shudder skidded through Rebecca's body. At first she labeled it as loathing. No, she corrected herself, not quite able to tear her gaze from the man, she was coming down with something. A spring cold, she decided. She felt dizzy, weak, feverish, and chilled at the same time. She definitely felt a cold coming on. She stubbornly refused to accept the fact that the symptoms had appeared the instant Jace Cooper had hobbled back into her life after nearly seven years. He couldn't have that kind of effect on her, not after all this time.

"Dominique or Max can work with him, or he can go elsewhere. I don't want anything to do with him."

"Why not?" Dr. Cornish asked in a West Texas drawl that sounded very out of place in Mishawaka, Indiana. Already he had given up acting tough. Rebecca knew it just wasn't in him. Donald Cornish was by nature an amiable sort.

Why not, he'd asked. She glanced away once again.

This time her gaze ran head-on into a pair of dark blue eyes. Why not? There were a million reasons she didn't want Jace Cooper as a patient, a million reasons she never wanted to see him again. There was a reason to go with each piece of the heart he had so thoroughly broken seven years ago.

Her logical, analytical mind was shocked at how fresh, how sharp, the pain seemed. She wasn't the kind of person who nursed a grudge, but seeing Jace again had wrenched open a door to the past she would rather have left nailed shut.

"Rebecca, do you have any idea who that is?" Cornish asked in a plaintive tone. "That's Jace Cooper, third baseman for the Chicago Kings. Do you have any idea how I *love* the Kings?"

"Donald, I don't want to hear about your personal perversions," she said with a hint of the dry humor he was used to hearing from her. "Take them up to the fifth floor. I'm sure Dr. Baxter could make room for you on his couch. As for Jace Cooper, I don't give a rat's posterior what he does. I'm too busy to work him into my schedule."

"I suppose it doesn't matter to you that he's going to be playing with the Mavericks until he gets himself back in top form. Do you know what that could mean to the Mavericks, your own hometown team?"

Her expression clearly told him exactly how much it meant to her. "Then let the Mavericks take care of him."

"You know full well the Mavericks' idea of a knowledgeable trainer is a guy whose brother used to empty bedpans at the VA hospital." Dr. Cornish affected a somewhat resigned air as he took a step away from Rebecca and shoved his hands into the pockets of his brown trousers. "Mr. Cooper specifically requested you as his therapist."

"Well, tough. Tell Mr. Cooper that for once in his life he isn't going to get what he wants. There are hundreds of qualified physical therapists in Chicago. I can't believe he found them all so unsatisfactory that he had to come here and bother me."

The door to her office swung open, and the object of her scorn hobbled in. The years hadn't altered his physique, she noted with grudging admiration. He wasn't a man of intimidating size, yet even on crutches Jace radiated an athletic energy that charged the air around him.

He had the kind of lean, rangy build that lent itself well to his profession. The well-muscled shoulders and upper arms that were now encased in a soft pink polo shirt gave him the power to swing a bat with authority. His slender waist and muscular legs, now hiding beneath a snug pair of jeans, gave him agility and speed on the infield. Baseball couldn't have custom-ordered a more perfect body for its needs.

Then Rebecca's gaze came to rest on the Lenox-Hill derotation brace he wore. It began at midthigh on his left leg, where his pant leg had been cut off to accommodate the metal and elastic device, and ended below his knee. A pain twisted in her chest. She looked away. No, she didn't want to know what had happened. He wasn't going to be her patient, therefore she didn't need to know. Even as she felt his unwanted allure take hold of her attention, she told herself she didn't want anything to do with this man, ever again.

"I know I'm barging in," Jace said. He watched Rebecca from the corner of his eye as he flashed a dazzling smile at Dr. Cornish. "But it is my body you're discussing. Hope you don't mind if I sit in."

"I do mind," Rebecca said tightly as she watched him ease himself down on the chrome-and-black-vinyl chair.

"Rebecca!" Dr. Cornish said in a lightly admonishing tone. He slouched down on the other chair in front of her desk and grinned at Jace like the village idiot. "Jace has every right to be in on this discussion."

She gave the doctor a stern look. He was as transparent as plate glass. Obviously he believed she wouldn't refuse the request with Jace sitting right there. Men. They always managed to stick together.

"Jace was telling me you worked with him before on a rather severe shoulder injury. He was very satisfied with the outcome."

"It was a slight separation," she said, crossing her arms over her chest and trying to look in command of the situation. "I followed the basic therapy routine. It was hardly on the scale of Lazarus being raised from the dead."

Jace sat back in his chair and smiled. If she remembered his slight injury after all these years, he had reason to hope. In his blacker moments since the accident, he had wondered if she would remember him at all. Seven years was a long time, and Rebecca Bradshaw was a very attractive lady. He had held out little hope that she would still be single, but the accommodating Dr. Cornish had informed him that Rebecca was indeed still eligible. That raised some interesting questions in his mind, but they were questions that were going to have to wait.

"Well," he said, giving her a little smile, "I was certainly impressed."

She merely stared at him. One thing hadn't changed in seven years—the lady still had a look that could freeze the Equator.

Jace took a deep breath and forged onward. "That was why I asked Dr. Cornish if you could be my therapist for this knee business."

"I'm afraid that's impossible, Mr. Cooper," she said

in her most businesslike tone, ignoring the sudden jump her heart rate had taken at his rogue's smile. "As director of the department, I have a great many administrative duties. My patient load is restricted to very special cases. I can assure you, you don't qualify."

Dr. Cornish leaned forward and offered Jace a lemon drop from the dish on Rebecca's desk. He took one himself and popped it into his mouth, then directed his steady brown gaze at the recalcitrant therapist. "I'm certain we can arrange something."

"And I'm certain we can't," Rebecca said. "I hope Mr. Cooper can understand that I have responsibilities I can't simply walk away from."

Jace barely managed to keep from wincing. Something else hadn't changed in seven years—the lady still had a tongue that could draw blood. At least she wasn't indifferent to him. He knew there was a fine line between anger and passion. If she still harbored one toward him, maybe she harbored the other as well. He was determined to find out one way or the other.

Just as Dr. Cornish opened his mouth to argue, the hospital page summoned him to the front desk. He hustled out of the office. Rebecca thought he must have taken all the air with him. She was suddenly alone with Jace the Ace, and she couldn't think of a single thing to say.

Jace lifted a manila folder thick with medical records and held it out toward her. "Will you at least take a look at my file?"

Something in his expression tugged at her. She denied the feeling but went on looking at him. It wasn't quite the face she remembered. At twenty-three he had been almost too handsome. He'd possessed the golden-boy looks to go along with his image. Now his face was a testimony to hard living. Age and experience had etched lines here and there. He had the same aquiline nose, the same stubborn chin and sensuously sculpted mouth, but the youthful bloom had faded, leaving him looking harder, more dangerous. Then there were his old-looking eyes. They seemed a little sad, a little tired.

Rebecca felt her resolve sway but told herself she was only giving in to him out of normal professional courtesy. She would look at his file and refer him to one of her other therapists, if she couldn't get rid of him altogether.

She reached out for the file. Their fingertips brushed. Rebecca jerked back as if she'd just grabbed hold of an electric cattle prod. The file dropped to the floor and sent papers scattering. She swore under her breath as she stooped to scoop them up.

What was the matter with her? Jace Cooper had given up his right to have any effect on her long ago. She wanted to demonstrate that to him with her coolness. So far she'd managed to dump hardware all over the floor of the exercise room, and now she'd carpeted her office with his medical records. So much for being cool.

"Need any help?" Jace asked as he bent over, his face only inches from hers.

She stared, suddenly mesmerized by his beautifully shaped mouth. She didn't remember his having that small scar angling away from his upper lip, but she could remember with startling clarity how that lip had tasted, how it had tempted her and teased her, how it had felt against her mouth, against her skin. Her breath grew short as her breasts grew heavy.

"No," she said, a jagged edge of panic inching into her voice. She jerked away from him and slammed her head into the edge of her desk. "Ouch!"

Rubbing the sore spot with one hand, she clumsily scraped up the last of the papers. Cradling the pile in the crook of one arm, she retreated to the chair behind her desk. Dammit, she said to herself, if he didn't leave soon, she was going to end up with a concussion.

Jace propped an elbow on the arm of his chair and rubbed his hand across his mouth to hide his smile. He knew for a fact that Rebecca would not appreciate him seeing humor in the situation.

He remained quiet for a moment as he watched her. He could almost see her willing her composure back into place as she read over his file, her brilliant green eyes framed by a pair of large black-rimmed reading glasses. Even seven years before, she had worn a mantle of self-possession the way a queen would wear an ermine-trimmed cloak. The only trouble had been that Rebecca's cloak had regularly slipped off one shoulder. She had never managed to be quite as aloof as she had wanted to be. She'd had too much warmth in her, too much caring to pull off the ice princess role. Then, too, there had been her penchant for dropping things and bumping into things when she got nervous. He still found that little quirk endearing.

It was damn good to see her again. The feeling was so strong, it almost startled him. Over the years he had never quite forgotten her, but it had been only since the accident that her image had become so clear in his mind. During his stay in the hospital he had begun to think of her often, to wonder what had become of her, to wonder if she ever thought of him.

In those weeks a lot of things had come into focus for him—the mistakes he'd made, the opportunities he had squandered, the precious treasure he'd once held in his hands and then casually tossed aside. The time had come to set some of those indiscretions to rights. Rebecca Bradshaw was where he needed to start.

He wanted to rebuild their relationship from the ground up. He needed to show her she could give her heart to him without fear of his breaking it again.

Where the relationship would ultimately go, he wasn't certain. Why it was so important to him it kept him awake at night, he couldn't quite say. He only knew he had to connect his life to hers once again in a deep and basic way.

As she turned one page of his file over and studied the next, Jace studied her. Seven years ago she had been a lovely girl, tall and willowy with a sense of fragility lying just under the surface, a vulnerability she hadn't quite been able to hide from him with her serious, studious expression. She had matured into a beautiful woman. A shock of black bangs was brushed up off her forehead, adding length to her rectangular face. Artfully applied makeup subtly emphasized her high cheekbones and the slight hollows beneath them.

A coat of sheer gloss drew his gaze to her mouth. It looked every bit as soft as he remembered, every bit as alluring. It was a very French mouth, something she had inherited from her mother. Her lips often fell into a sultry pout that was not in the least affected but was perfectly natural and incredibly sexy. He could remember the taste of that mouth, the texture, the way it had whispered his name in passion.

As arousal began to settle blood in his groin, Jace cleared his throat and asked, "How's your father?"

Rebecca didn't look up even though she wasn't comprehending a bit of what she was staring at. "He's fine."

"And your sister—ah—Ellen, right?"

She hesitated, her fingers automatically clenching and unclenching the pen she held in her left hand. "Fine." At least she hadn't heard any differently.

"I've missed you," Jace said, surprising himself. Where had that come from? Not that it mattered. Rebecca wasn't about to believe it.

"Right," she said, covering her vulnerability with a

derisive laugh. "I read that between the lines in all those letters you never wrote me."

Jace sucked in a long breath between his teeth and let it out slowly, wishing he had a cigarette.

With an effort Rebecca pushed all disturbing thoughts aside and forced herself to concentrate on her job. Her highly efficient, highly intelligent brain absorbed and processed the technical terms on the page in front of her. "So this wasn't a sports' injury?"

"No. Car accident." He still couldn't say those two words without feeling a stab of guilt and remorse.

"According to this, you were receiving excellent care in Chicago. Why change horses in the middle of the stream?"

"I didn't have much of a choice," he said, unable to keep some of the bitterness from his voice. "The Kings' management sent me down here. I'll be playing with the Mavericks once I get this old hinge working again. The sooner, the better. With a little luck and a lot of hard work, I'll get called back to Chicago before the end of the season."

"I see." So he was planning his great escape from the rustic provinces already, and he hadn't even been here a day yet. Same old Jace. He was no doubt champing at the bit to get back to the bright lights and big city. Rebecca told herself she was glad. The only thing that could have been better was if he hadn't shown up at all.

"You're head of the department already, huh?" he commented, glancing around her orderly white-walled office. Framed diplomas and award certificates hung on the wall behind her. A thriving English ivy plant trailed over the edge of its pot and crept down the side of a black cabinet. "You've done well for yourself, Becca."

"Thank you." She ignored the twinge his nickname

for her caused and tried to focus on the notes his previous therapist had made.

"You cut your hair," he said softly, mesmerized by the way the straight glossy mass swayed as she moved her head. He remembered when it had been so long, he'd had to nuzzle through the silky tresses to find her nipples. His voice dropped a note as he said, "I liked it long."

Rebecca forced her heart down out of her throat as she tried to block out the memory of him lifting the curtain of black over her shoulder so he could kiss her breast. Why should she care whether he noticed her haircut or liked it or not? "Yes, well, you weren't around for a consultation when I decided to cut it off."

He let her sarcastic remark slide. "I like it. It makes you look very sophisticated."

The comment was right on target, whether Jace realized it or not. She had parted with her long tresses just after Jace's departure, partly for symbolic reasons. Idealistic, romantic girls had long hair. Practical, sophisticated women did not.

Rebecca heaved an impatient sigh and stabbed him with a pointed look. "Thank you, Vidal Sassoon. Now, can we please get on with the evaluation of your knee?"

He shrugged affably. "Sure."

The injury to his knee had been serious, she noted. Cartilage had been torn and ligaments had been damaged. It had been severe enough to require major surgery rather than the more common arthroscopic surgery. It wasn't so serious an injury that Jace would be left permanently crippled, but it was severe enough to make an athlete seriously consider retirement.

"According to what I'm reading here, you'll have your work cut out to regain the kind of mobility you need to play major league baseball. The knee will always be susceptible to heavy stress, meaning it could go on you again if you don't maintain a rigid exercise program or if you try to use it too soon." She looked up from the papers with serious eyes. "You're past your prime, athletically speaking. Why don't you retire?"

He'd heard the same question from his other doctors and therapists. He'd heard it from teammates and the team management. Apparently no one believed he was capable of coming back. They couldn't seem to understand his need to come back, his need to prove to himself that he had what it took to work for a dream instead of sitting back and waiting to have it dropped into his lap. He'd been that kind of man once, the kind who took his good fortune for granted—but those days were over.

"I need to prove something."

"To your adoring fans?" Rebecca questioned, arching a black brow.

"To myself," he said quietly. "Fans aren't very adoring once you fall out of the limelight."

He wasn't the old Jace Cooper. Somehow the thought unnerved Rebecca. The Jace she remembered had had a boundless belief in his own popularity. He had been a horrible patient because he had believed he was entitled to a perfect body. He hadn't wanted to work for it. He had been the type who floated through life on a wealth of charm and talent, but charm and talent wouldn't help him now.

"Getting that knee into shape will require a great deal of hard work, sweat, and pain," she declared.

Jace flashed her one of his patented smiles. "No pain, no gain. Does this mean you've changed your mind about taking me on as a patient?"

"No. Even if I could work you into my schedule, I wouldn't. I don't think it would be a good idea for us to work together."

Jace pushed himself out of his chair, braced his

hands on Rebecca's desk top, and leaned over her, a keen watchfulness lighting his dark blue eyes. "Are you saying that after nearly seven years, you're still so angry with me that you can't be objective enough to treat me?"

Rebecca bristled. "Of course not. I don't feel anything for you."

"Liar," he said with a good-natured chuckle, not the least offended by her claim. It was a load of garbage. He was willing to bet his house on that—if he hadn't already lost it to the tax man and if he hadn't given up gambling. "Ever since I came through the front door, you've been as nervous as the proverbial cat in the room full of rocking chairs. Admit it, Becca."

She shifted uncomfortably on her chair. Why did he have to get so darn close to her? The scent of his aftershave was having some weird kind of numbing effect on her brain and respiratory system. "I admit you caught me off balance. You're the last person I expected to see walk into my therapy department."

"So you're saying what's past is past? Then why won't you work with me?"

"I told you," she said, dodging his gaze and trying to take in oxygen without breathing in his clean male scent. "I can't fit you into my schedule."

"That's it? That's the only reason?"

Sick of his bullying, she glared up at him. "I don't like you. That's reason enough."

"I'll bet you don't like a lot of your patients," Jace speculated, trying not to let the sweet allure of her perfume distract him from the conversation. "You can hardly pick and choose the kind of people who get into accidents or develop debilitating diseases. I'm sure you get your share of jerks here."

Rebecca pushed her chair back from her desk and rose to her full height, which nearly equaled Jace's.

"Yes, I do get my share of jerks here, and I have no intention of adding your name to the head of that list. If you want to take your therapy in this hospital, you'll take it with whomever I say."

"If you don't feel anything for me, why can't it be you?"

He was pressing his luck, pushing her this way. Lord knew he'd made enough mistakes with Becca. But it was plain she was going to retreat, that she would simply avoid him rather than be confronted with a painful reminder of the past.

He couldn't let that happen. Somehow he felt that his whole future hinged on making a fresh start with Rebecca Bradshaw. He couldn't accomplish that if she was never around, so he threw out a challenge. "I think you're afraid, Becca. I think the thought of working closely with me scares you, because you've realized you do feel something for me, even after all these years."

She pulled her reading glasses off and threw them onto her desk. "Yes, you're right, I do feel something. Loathing, contempt, anger. I would have denied it yesterday, but seeing you has brought it all back to me. I thought I had put those feelings aside years ago, because, frankly, you aren't worth the wasted effort. But I guess they've lain dormant since I never had the chance to vent them on you. A person doesn't get a lot of satisfaction out of railing at someone who's vanished into thin air."

Well, you asked for that, Jace, old boy, he thought, straightening from the desk. As he propped one hand on his hip, he ran the other through his hair. He sighed and glanced out the window to the exercise room, where he could see a striking, statuesque therapist showing an elderly woman how to use a walker.

He'd hurt Rebecca when he'd left Mishawaka for Chicago, but he hadn't realized just how deeply he'd hurt her. To think that she could still hate him for it after all this time cut him to the quick.

Lord, what a bastard he'd been. Rebecca had been so sweet, so giving. She had trusted him with secret fears and hopes she had never shared with anyone else. But when his shot at the big leagues had come, he'd walked away without a backward glance. He'd been so caught up in his own success, he'd packed up and gone without giving her anything more than a quick phone call to say good-bye.

When he turned back to her, there was pain in his eyes that had nothing to do with his injured knee. "I'm sorry I hurt you, Becca."

"Thank you," she said, combing her raven hair back behind one ear. She was angry with herself for confessing her feelings to Jace. Still, she couldn't help adding, "Seven years after the fact."

His dark brows bobbed above his eyes as he mustered a sad smile. What excuse could he offer? There was none. "Better late than never."

"Better not at all." Rebecca shook her head, which had begun to pound from tension and from having knocked it into the parallel bar and her desk. She stared down at her shoes and resigned herself to making another admission. "I wish you hadn't come back here, Jace."

"That's honest." It hurt, but it was honest. "I'll be honest too. Life has come full circle for me, Becca. I've done a lot of things I'm not proud of. I've wasted a lot of opportunities. I haven't been the kind of person I should have been. I could have been killed in that accident, but I wasn't. For whatever reason, God saw fit to save my miserable hide. I've been given another chance, and I'm going to make the most of it."

He looked at her with the kind of hawkish determination she remembered seeing on his face when he was on the baseball diamond.

"I'm going to fight my way back from this knee injury—with or without your help," he said. "I'm going to make it back to the majors—with or without the support of the Kings' management. And I'm going to win you back, Rebecca Bradshaw—whether you like it or not."

Two

A chill went through her. Whether it was fear or anticipation, Rebecca couldn't have said. She stared at Jace Cooper as if she was certain he had taken complete leave of the little sense she credited him with. "That's absurd! You can't have a relationship with someone who isn't interested in you."

"You were interested once," he pointed out. He was a little shocked himself by the claim he'd made. He hadn't planned on blurting it out that way, but he wasn't going to back down. The idea of not only clearing the slate with Becca but also renewing the relationship they'd shared felt right, dead-solid perfect—like a hit that sailed over the left field fence before he could even let go of the bat.

"That was a long time ago," Rebecca said, not liking the gleam in his eyes.

"It wasn't so long ago that we've forgotten how good it was between us."

Jace cursed his bum knee. If he had been more mobile, Rebecca wouldn't have been able to hide from him behind her desk. He would have joined her back there, and he might have made good on the promise he was sure was in his eyes, the promise to refresh her memory. Damn, but he was aching to kiss her!

As if she sensed that, Rebecca backed away warily. She shook her head at the memories and at Jace's idea. "I don't want you, Jace. I don't like you, and I don't trust you."

"I don't blame you, honey," he said truthfully, "but I'm not the same man who hurt you, Becca. I've changed, and I intend to prove it to you."

"You'll be wasting your time."

He smiled as he perched a hip on one corner of her desk and picked up her round glass paperweight. He tested the feel of it in his hand and fleetingly wished it were a baseball. "I don't think so."

Rebecca rarely lost her temper, but now she was fuming. She literally saw red as she stared at Jace. "You arrogant jackass! If you think for one minute that you can just waltz back into my life after seven years and pick up where you left off, you're out of your mind! I won't be your little plaything while you bide your time waiting to get called back to the big leagues! I can't believe even you would have the flaming arrogance to make that kind of assumption."

She stormed past him but paused with her hand on the doorknob to deliver a parting shot. "Maybe women back in Chicago line up, eager to fall at your feet—and no doubt that will happen here as well—but I won't be among them!"

Rebecca swung her office door open and ran head-on into Dr. Cornish.

She backed away from the door as the head administrator followed Dr. Cornish in.

"Rebecca," Dr. Cornish said with an unrepentant

grin. "I ran into Mr. Saunders downstairs. He was eager to meet Jace."

"Yes, I was," Saunders said, his pleasant smile revealing neatly capped teeth. He was a distinguished-looking older man whose passion for athletics showed in his youthful looking physique. "I have to tell you, Mr. Cooper, our little hospital may not have the prestige you're used to, but you couldn't put your knee in better hands than Rebecca's. She's a topflight physical therapist. I'm proud to say the Mayo Clinic tried to lure her away from us. We're damn lucky to have her." He shot a sweetly apologetic look at Rebecca. "Pardon my French, Rebecca."

She couldn't help but smile at him, even if he was infatuated with Jace. He was practically a second father to her.

Saunders' sudden frown was very much that of a disapproving parent. "Donald tells me there's some question as to whether or not you'll work with Mr. Cooper."

"You know I try to limit my caseload to severe problems, Mr. Saunders. Mr. Cooper's injury really isn't so serious."

"It's serious enough to threaten his career."

It was the same tone of voice her father had always used when he was about to ground her sister, Ellen. Mr. Saunders could just as well have tagged "young lady" onto the end of his sentence.

Rebecca drew in a deep breath and glanced out the window. Bob Wilkes was making the rounds in his wheelchair, giving words of encouragement to other patients. As an idea took shape, a smile began to tug at the corners of her mouth.

She turned back to the administrator just as he launched into a lecture.

"As Mr. Cooper has specifically sought our help in

this matter, I feel it our duty to give him the very best we have to offer— "

"Yes, I agree."

Three pairs of eyes stared at her in surprise.

Jace was the first to speak. "You've changed your mind? You'll work with me?"

Rebecca smiled broadly then. She would work with him. She would be his unrelenting taskmaster. She would show Jace Cooper she was a woman of steely resolve, that she could face him on a daily basis and not be the least affected by his famous charm. And if he did pursue the idea of renewing his old relationship with her, she would be able to shake her head and tell him she didn't date patients—*ever.*

"Yes," she said, glancing back out the window as Susie Chin rolled into the exercise room in her wheelchair. "Now, if you'll excuse me, gentlemen, I see my next patient has arrived. This is to be her first day at the parallel bars, and I'm sure she's nervous. I don't want to keep her waiting."

When she started for the door, Jace blocked her path. His expression was wary. He was obviously trying to puzzle out her sudden change of heart.

"Thank you, Becca," he said softly.

"That'll be the last time you thank me. I expect you to be here at eight o'clock sharp tomorrow morning, ready and willing to work your butt off."

The corners of his clear-cut lips tipped up as he gave her a brief salute and hopped out of her way. "Aye, aye, ma'am."

Rebecca slumped onto her chair, feeling as worn out as an old rag doll. She propped her elbows on the desk and rubbed the last of her makeup off her face with her hands. What a day.

Physical therapy was a demanding profession. Helping to lift and move patients was hard physical work. Taking a patient from evaluation through the final stages of rehabilitation was mentally and emotionally demanding as well. Yet this was what she had wanted to do since she'd been a little girl. Watching her mother struggle with the debilitating effects of amyotrophic lateral sclerosis—Lou Gehrig's disease—had inspired her to her career, and she loved it. Most of the time.

"Here," Dominique said, as she walked into the office and set a bottle of lemon-flavored mineral water in front of Rebecca. She lowered herself into a chair on the other side of the desk, stretched out her mile-long legs, and propped her feet up on the wastebasket. "It's not exactly a piña colada, but we can always pretend, can't we?"

"Yes," Rebecca said with a sigh. "I feel as if I've been put through one of those old wringer washing machines."

"Must have been all that time you spent in here with Jace Cooper." Dominique's dark eyes sparkled. "I admit to feeling a little weak in the knees myself. What was that big powwow all about?"

Rebecca grimaced. "The Great Railroad Conspiracy. I have been duly chosen by the powers that be to oversee Mr. Cooper's therapy since he's going to be such a valuable member of the community now."

"Was it his good looks that turned you off or the fact that he's got more charisma than Tom Cruise and Dennis Quaid put together?"

"I used to know Jace Cooper."

"Are we talking 'know' as in the biblical sense?" Dominique asked.

Rebecca nodded.

"I'll work with him," Dominique said resolutely. "To hell with Griffith Saunders."

"Thanks, pal," Rebecca said with a warm smile. The offer was a tempting one, but she had made her mind up. "But no thanks. I gave it some thought, and I believe the best thing I can do is work with Jace. What better way to show him I'm immune to him than to face him head-on without flinching?"

"Oh . . ." Mischief lit Dominique's dark face. "You could line his athletic cup with an itch weed potion. I'll call my mother and get her recipe. Her grandfather was a medicine man, you know."

Rebecca laughed, feeling the day's problems lift a bit off her shoulders. She pushed herself to her feet and said, "Let's call it a day. I just want to go home, eat a pizza, and crash."

She would have added "forget Jace Cooper" to that list, but Rebecca Bradshaw was nothing if not practical. With their next confrontation looming on the horizon, there was little chance she would be able to forget about him overnight.

Rebecca went to the parking lot with her spring coat slung over her arm. As she unlocked the door of her blue Honda Accord, Rebecca took a deep, cleansing breath. Maybe the day had been awful, but the grass was still growing and the sun would come up tomorrow. One thing she had learned—life could be hard, but the world went on turning and people made it from day to day.

All things considered, she didn't have such a tough row to hoe. It was just that at the moment, her row had a big rock in it—Jace Cooper. Rocks could be moved. In Jace's case they rolled away and gathered no moss.

Rebecca didn't let herself wonder why it stung a little to think he would only be there to pester her until greener pastures lured him away again.

As she pulled her car out of the hospital parking lot

and headed for home, she stuck a tape in the tape deck and settled back with a sigh and a smile. The strains of Pachelbel's Canon in D floated from the speakers. The full round tones of peace and serenity filled the car. Violins sang a serenade to the end of a beautiful spring day. Rebecca felt her tension drift away on the soothing tide of sound.

A lone figure moving down the tree-lined sidewalk caught her eye. A lone figure swinging slowly along on crutches. Before her mind could register who it was, her heart was already picking up a new rhythm. She drew even with Jace, who was trudging along with a huge duffel bag strapped across his back. Rebecca sighed and pulled her car over to the curb. Jace glanced at her and then had the audacity to appear surprised.

"Just what do you think you're doing?" Rebecca yelled as she slid across to the passenger seat and stuck her head out the window.

"Heading home." He put on his little-lost-boy look. "Providing I can find it."

If he thought he was going to play on her sympathy, he was sadly mistaken. Rebecca wasn't about to fall for that routine. "We have taxicabs, you know. They're not exclusive to Chicago."

"Mmm," he said noncommittally as he glanced around. "It's a nice day for a walk."

"You're not walking, you're hobbling," she pointed out, all her mother hen instincts rushing to the fore in spite of her resolve to take no pity on him. He should have been sitting somewhere with that knee elevated and packed with a warm compress. Knowing him, he'd probably been on it all day. "How far are you going?"

Jace shrugged with a comically innocent expression on his handsome face. "I'm not sure I remember my way around that well."

"What's the address?" she asked impatiently.

He dug a hand into the front pocket of his jeans, stressing fabric that was already under considerable strain. Rebecca swallowed hard as unwanted memories washed over her in a hot flash. He was a beautifully built man in every respect, and his athleticism had never been confined to the baseball diamond. It made her furious to admit to herself that no man had ever measured up to Jace Cooper in bed, but that was the plain truth.

She couldn't help breathing a sigh of relief when his hand emerged with a crumpled scrap of paper, but all the blood drained out of her face as he read the address he had scribbled down.

"That's Muriel Marquardt's house," she said weakly. "That's right across the alley from my house."

Jace's dark eyes rounded. "Is it?"

Rebecca scowled at him, her elegant hand curling into a fist on the open window of the car. "You know darn well it is!"

He didn't deny it. She wouldn't have believed him if he had. This was vintage Jace Cooper—an all-out assault. She shouldn't have been the least surprised. After all, he had very clearly stated his intentions. Well, if he thought living in close proximity was somehow going to weaken her resolve and make her susceptible to his charm, he was deluding himself. She was going to ignore him on every plane but the professional . . . just as soon as she took him home . . . to the house that stood directly behind her own.

"Get in the car. Get in the car!" she said in a tight voice.

Propping his crutches against the side of Rebecca's Honda, Jace shrugged off his duffel bag and tossed it into the back seat. Gingerly, he eased himself into the car, bad leg first, so he wouldn't have to bend the knee that had begun to swell and ache. He buckled his seat belt as soon as he closed the door, and he glanced across to make certain Rebecca had hers in place as well.

Rebecca didn't say a word until she signaled and pulled away from the curb. "You're some kind of crazy person. You always were a little off the mark, but you're in the deep end of the pool now. Don't try to tell me you didn't plan this well in advance, Jace Cooper. Don't try to tell me you didn't."

"Gee, Becca," he said mildly, rubbing at the ache in the muscle above his sore knee, "are you upset? You're repeating yourself. I remember you used to do that when you were upset."

She halted the car at a red light and took advantage of the opportunity to glare at him, her eyes narrowed to mere slits. She didn't speak again until the light changed. "How did you get Mrs. Marquardt's name? She hasn't been advertising for a boarder."

"Ummm . . . a friend gave her name to me," he said evasively, fixing his gaze on the bus they were passing.

Rebecca was too steamed to notice his strange tone of voice. So he had friends in Mishawaka, did he? He hadn't bothered to do so much as send her a Christmas card in seven years, but he had friends here who could line up accommodations for him at a moment's notice. Wasn't that just peachy?

Well, she thought, half chuckling to herself, maybe they weren't such good friends after all. A room at Muriel Marquardt's house wasn't going to be quite what Jace was used to.

"Renting a room from an elderly lady is hardly your style," she commented as she negotiated a right turn that took them into an older residential area where the houses were big and sturdy and full-grown maple and oak trees lined the boulevard. "I would ask why you didn't have this famous friend of yours find you a posh

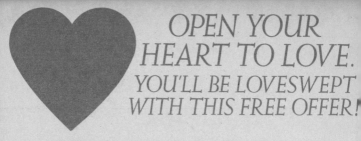

OPEN YOUR HEART TO LOVE.
YOU'LL BE LOVESWEPT WITH THIS FREE OFFER!

HERE'S WHAT YOU GET:

1. **FREE! SIX NEW LOVESWEPT NOVELS!** You get 6 beautiful stories filled with passion, romance, laughter, and tears...exciting romances to stir the excitement of falling in love... again and again.

2. **FREE! A BEAUTIFUL MAKEUP CASE WITH A MIRROR THAT LIGHTS UP!**
What could be more useful than a makeup case with a mirror that lights up*? Once you open the tortoise-shell finish case, you have a choice of brushes...for your lips, your eyes, and your blushing cheeks.
*(batteries not included)

3. **SAVE! MONEY-SAVING HOME DELIVERY!** Join the Loveswept at-home reader service and we'll send you 6 new novels each month. You always get 15 days to preview them before you decide. Each book is yours for only $2.09 — a savings of 41¢ per book.

4. **BEAT THE CROWDS!** You'll always receive your Loveswept books before they are available in bookstores. You'll be the first to thrill to these exciting new stories.

BE LOVESWEPT TODAY — JUST COMPLETE, DETACH AND MAIL YOUR FREE-OFFER CARD.

FREE–LIGHTED MAKEUP CASE!
FREE–6 LOVESWEPT NOVELS!

- NO OBLIGATION
- NO PURCHASE NECESSARY

(DETACH AND MAIL CARD TODAY.)

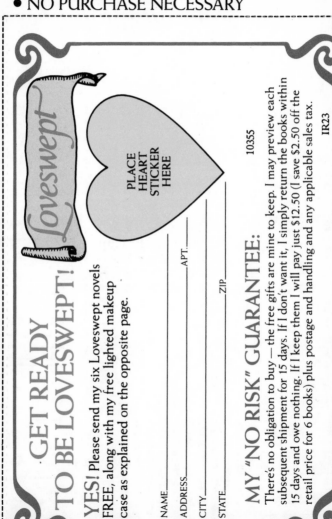

GET READY TO BE LOVESWEPT!

YES! Please send my six Loveswept novels FREE, along with my free lighted makeup case as explained on the opposite page.

PLACE HEART STICKER HERE

Loveswept

NAME_____

ADDRESS_____APT._____

CITY_____

STATE_____ZIP_____

10355

IR23

MY "NO RISK" GUARANTEE:

There's no obligation to buy — the free gifts are mine to keep. I may preview each subsequent shipment for 15 days. If I don't want it, I simply return the books within 15 days and owe nothing. If I keep them I will pay just $12.50 (I save $2.50 off the retail price for 6 books) plus postage and handling and any applicable sales tax.

REMEMBER!

- The free books and gift are mine to keep!
- There is no obligation!
- I may preview each shipment for 15 days!
- I can cancel anytime!

(DETACH AND MAIL CARD TODAY.)

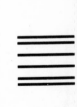

BUSINESS REPLY MAIL

FIRST-CLASS MAIL   PERMIT NO. 2456   HICKSVILLE, NY.

POSTAGE WILL BE PAID BY ADDRESSEE

Loveswept

Bantam Books
P.O. Box 985
Hicksville, NY 11802-9827

NO POSTAGE
NECESSARY
IF MAILED
IN THE
UNITED STATES

condo overlooking the river, but I've realized this is part of your demented scheme."

She was right. It was part of his master plan, but that wasn't the only reason he'd taken a room in a less-than-fashionable part of town. Jace wondered what Rebecca would have to say if he told her he couldn't afford much better at the moment. He could well imagine the tongue-lashing he'd get if he told her he'd gambled away a good deal of his money.

He glanced at her. She was muttering to herself under her breath as she hit the turn signal with a ruthless motion that threatened to break the slender wand. Obviously she was in no mood to hear the story of the last seven years of his life. She looked more ready to put an end to his life.

That fact would have discouraged him if not for her reaction to him that afternoon. No woman got that skittish around a man she cared nothing about. If he meant nothing to her, she would long since have let go of the hurt and anger his leaving had caused.

"I'll admit it," he said. "You have an IQ of two hundred plus. It's not likely that I could come up with a plan so subtle you couldn't figure it out, so why not be obvious about it? I mean to set the past to rights with you, Becca. It'll just save me a lot of time and trouble if we're in the same neighborhood."

"Oh, yes, by all means!" she said. "Why go to a lot of extra trouble? I might as well be handy!"

"Becca, that's not how I meant it." His thinning patience was evident in his tone of voice. Just enough steel came through the flannel softness to warn her she wasn't the only one who'd had a long day. She'd pushed him about as far as he was going to allow. Yes, he deserved her sarcasm. Yes, he'd expected a show of temper. But he wasn't going to be a martyr about it.

Rebecca took her gaze off the road just long enough

to glimpse the stern look on his face—a look that quickly turned to a grimace of pain as one of her front tires dropped into a pothole. With a cry of pain, he squeezed his eyes shut and grabbed his injured knee.

"Oh, Jace! I'm sorry!" She swerved the car to the curb and slammed it into park. Leaning across his crutches, she reached for his leg, gently pushing his hand away and replacing it with her own. "Lean back and try to relax. Tensing up the muscles will only prolong the pain."

Jace gasped for air as he forced himself to sit back. The pain that had driven into his knee like red-hot pokers gradually receded as Rebecca gently massaged his thigh. It felt like heaven, even through the heavy elasticized brace he wore. A feeling of weakness shivered through him as he relaxed.

"Better?" she questioned softly, her hand steadily kneading the cramped muscle.

He nodded, his head falling back against the plush gray seat.

"You've been on it too much today, haven't you?"

"I guess." The bus ride from Chicago hadn't done it any good either, but he didn't feel much like talking about that at the moment.

"Does it feel as if it's swelling?"

"Like a balloon."

Rebecca clucked her disapproval. "You always were a horrible patient. As soon as we get you to Muriel's, I want you to elevate this knee and get some ice on it to take the swelling down, then go to a warm compress to stimulate blood flow. Did Dr. Cornish give you a prescription for pain pills?"

"I don't want any drugs."

"Jace, you're in pain—"

The look he gave her ended the argument as surely as his words did. "No drugs."

Rebecca raised her free hand in surrender. "Fine. No prescription drugs. But please, take some aspirin. That will help take the inflammation down as well as making you more comfortable. I doubt you'll be able to sleep tonight without it."

He nodded again as his body relaxed another degree. Pain in his knee wasn't the only thing that was going to keep him awake, he thought, biting back a moan. Rebecca continued to rub his thigh absently as she quizzed him about his injury. As if they had minds of their own, her fingers crept up under the frayed edge of the cutoff leg of his jeans. Flesh massaged flesh with no barrier to dull the pleasure. Jace let his imagination draw her hand upward an inch at a time.

He wanted her. He hadn't wanted a woman since the accident, nearly two months before, but he wanted Rebecca Bradshaw. Memories rushed back of the way she'd felt beneath him, around him. All the tastes and sounds and scents of her filled his mind until he had to fight them off as a matter of self-preservation. He had to remind himself that Rebecca was a long way from welcoming his advances, even if her fingers were doing a little reminiscing of their own.

Jace knew the instant she realized what she was doing. Her brilliant green eyes seemed to double in size. She jerked her hand from his leg and stared at it in a most accusatory way, as if it had betrayed her.

"Don't stop on my account," he said in a warm lazy voice.

His head lolled to one side as he watched her skitter across the seat until she was practically jammed up against the door on the driver's side. A blush rouged her cheeks. Jace chuckled. "Do you think aspirin will take care of the swelling in other parts of my anatomy?"

Conceited man! He undoubtedly thought she had

been touching him on purpose. "I doubt it will do anything for a swelled head," Rebecca said primly.

"It's not my head that's swelling at the moment."

It was on the tip of her tongue to tell him that maybe he shouldn't wear such tight pants, but she bit back the words. Remembrance shuddered through her and settled in a warm pool in the pit of her belly. She fixed her gaze on the odometer as she leaned forward to start the car. The Honda buzzed a noisy protest.

"You never turned it off," Jace pointed out unnecessarily.

Rebecca blushed a deep apple red. "Must you make everything into a sexual innuendo?"

"What did I say?" he asked with a shrug, amusement sparkling in his dark blue eyes. "Oh, you mean, turned off as opposed to turned on—the way I am right now?"

The Honda lurched backward. Rebecca muttered steadily under her breath as she rammed the gearshift and pressed down on the accelerator. The motor raced.

"That's neutral."

She shot him a withering glare. "Would you like to drive?"

Jace sobered and glanced away. "No."

Rebecca shifted on the seat uneasily as she managed to get the car into drive and eased it away from the curb. She felt as if she'd slapped a puppy. Jace's teasing was abruptly finished, and it was somehow her fault. Not that she had wanted him to tease her. It was just that this brooding silence wasn't like him.

"Was it a bad accident?" she asked cautiously, stealing a glance at him. He was staring out the side window, his shoulders tensed as if ready for a blow.

"Yes."

"Were you with—"

"I don't want to talk about it right now, Becca."

There was a certain urgency in his voice that caught

her interest and, at the same time, kept her from prob-
ing deeper. She focused on the quiet, tree-lined street
and piloted the car toward home. That was where she
wanted to be—home, in the house she'd grown up in.
Home, away from Jace Cooper. She was glad he had
ended the subject because she didn't want to know
anything about his life since she had ceased to be part
of it. It was none of her business.

She glanced at the digital clock nestled in among the
dashboard instruments and bit her lip. "I have to make
a quick stop at home before I take you to Muriel's."

"I can walk from your place. You said yourself it's
just across the alley."

She shot him her sternest health-care-professional
look. "No. You've walked enough for one day."

"I have to admit, it does feel good to sit here." He
grinned, his old good humor returning. "It felt even
better when you had your hand on my thigh."

Heat blossomed again under the surface of her fair
skin. "That won't happen any more," she said stiffly as
she signaled and pulled into the driveway of a sturdy
two-story house painted white with colonial blue shutters and trim.

"We'll see."

"I mean it, Jace," she said soberly. "I'm not getting
involved with you again."

"You're already involved."

"Professionally."

"That's a hard line to draw when you've already been
to bed with someone."

The shot was right on target. She should have congratulated him on his marksmanship. Instead she
turned the car off and yanked the keys from the ignition. The look she gave him walked a thin line between
hurt and hatred. Her voice trembled with emotion.
"Consider it drawn."

She swung her long legs out of the Honda and started up the sidewalk at a brisk pace. Jace hauled himself out on the passenger side and leaned against the roof. As he started to call out to her, the front door of the house opened and a miniature human cannonball launched himself off the front porch with an exuberant shout.

"Mom! Mom, guess what!"

Jace's jaw dropped. He felt as if he'd just been hit in the stomach with a medicine ball. *Mom?* Becca was a *mom?*

Justin's freckle-dusted face and gap-toothed grin was all Rebecca needed to see at the end of the day to revive her flagging spirits. Forgetting Jace Cooper, she dropped down to the sidewalk on her knees and held her arms out. Immediately they were filled with wriggling boy.

"Guess what what?" she asked, giggling as she hugged and was hugged in return.

"Peter Cleary brought a dead rat to school, and Jessica Jorgenson threw up at lunch."

Rebecca made a face and tousled the boy's dark hair. "Sounds as though you had quite a day."

"Uh-huh," he said, rocking back on the heels of his miniature high-top sneakers. He propped one hand on his hip and shoved the other into the deep pocket of his favorite camouflage pants. "Mrs. Petrie let us have extra time at recess, and I got a star on my spelling paper."

"That's super!" she said, giving him an extra hug. "I'm so proud of you! How did the arithmetic go today?" she asked carefully, knowing Justin was less than enthusiastic about first-grade math.

He made a face and glanced over her shoulder, his blue eyes widening as his gaze landed on Jace. Addition and subtraction were instantly forgotten. In an exaggerated stage whisper he said, "Who's that man by our car?"

Speech evaded Rebecca as she suddenly remembered Jace's presence. The joy she'd felt at seeing Justin suddenly jelled into a knot of tension in the middle of her chest.

Justin turned a very adult look of reprimand on her. "Don't ever give rides to strangers, Mom."

"Ah—um—Mr. Cooper isn't a stranger, honey." She pushed herself to a standing position and reluctantly led Justin by the hand to make what was bound to be an awkward introduction. Stopping a few feet from the car she said, "Mr. Cooper is an old—" The word "friend" stuck in her throat. Friends didn't simply abandon friends the way Jace had. "—person."

Justin tipped his head in speculation as he looked up at Jace. "You're not *so* old," he said candidly. "Grandpa's old. You're just kind of old—like Mom."

"Thanks," Rebecca said sardonically.

"Thanks," Jace mumbled, still dumbfounded by this living proof that Becca was a mom. He held his hand out. "Jace Cooper."

Pleased at being treated like an adult, Justin grinned and accepted the offer. "I'm Justin. I'm six."

The boy had Rebecca's black hair and rectangular face. His grin was filled with mischief. A smattering of rusty freckles dotted his cheeks and impudent button nose. And his eyes were a deep, bottomless blue.

Rebecca could practically hear the wheels turning in Jace's brain. It didn't take a mind reader to know he was making comparisons and doing some basic math. His still-startled gaze darted from Justin to her.

"Justin," she said, drawing her son back and steering him toward the house, "will you please go tell Grandpa I'll be a little late for supper? I have to drive

Mr. Cooper around the block to Mrs. Marquardt's house."

"Can I come along?" Justin asked automatically. He was always ready for an adventure.

"No, sweetheart. Go on now. I'll be back in a little while." Her gaze lingered on him as he scampered up the steps and dashed into the house, yelling at the top of his lungs.

"Becca?" Jace questioned.

Emotions warred inside her. Without turning around, she could picture Jace's expression. He didn't have to say anything more than her name for her to know the question that was burning inside him, between them.

"Rebecca?"

Wearing her pride like a cloak, she turned and looked him square in the eye. "He's not your son."

Three

"What do you mean, it's none of my business?" Jace asked indignantly.

"The statement is generally considered self-explanatory." Rebecca kept her eyes focused forward. She turned at the corner and gunned the engine more than was necessary for the Honda to negotiate the slight incline. The sooner she dumped Jace off, the sooner this conversation would be over. She'd had all she could take for one day. She wasn't about to discuss Justin with this man who had dropped back into her life as suddenly as he had left it.

"If I fathered a child, I have a right to know."

"I told you, you're not Justin's father."

Jace's temper rattled the lid on his control. Quelling the urge to reach over and shake the truth out of her, his blunt-tipped fingers bit into the arm rest. "Then who the hell is, and where the hell is he?"

"It's none of your business."

Rebecca turned in at the drive of a Victorian monstrosity with peeling brown paint. The place had a definite air of neglect about it. The lawn was trimmed, but the flower beds were brown patches of dirt studded with dried skeletons of plants. Cats scattered in all directions at the car's approach.

Jace barely glanced at his new residence. His attention remained riveted on the woman beside him. He remembered the tilt to her chin, the tightness around her lush mouth. Wild horses wouldn't drag the answer from her, but he would try. "Dammit, Rebecca, now see here—"

"No. Now you see here." She turned in her seat and jabbed a slender forefinger at him. "You can't question me about my personal life because my personal life doesn't concern you. You gave up all rights in that area seven years ago, Jace."

She climbed out of the car and opened the back door to lug Jace's duffel bag out of the backseat. It wasn't exactly light, but neither were the patients she lifted every day. Slinging the strap over her shoulder, she backed away from the car and shut the door before a big black cat could slip inside.

Jace hauled himself out of the compact, his concentration divided between his throbbing knee and getting the truth out of Rebecca. He couldn't decide which would be worse—finding out he had sired a son seven years ago and no one had bothered to tell him, or finding out Rebecca had given birth to another man's child.

Without a word to him, she turned and started up the winding sidewalk to the front porch of the imposing house. He hobbled after her, dodging a pair of tiger-striped kittens who seemed to think crutches were great fun to play with.

"I know you're not married, and I don't think you're divorced," he said, catching up to her. "So what's the story? Either Justin is my son and you're flat-out lying to me, or you met some other man when you were on the rebound."

Rebecca paused at the foot of the steps and gave him a look as she adjusted the shoulder strap of the duffel. "*All My Children* could have used you during the writers' strike."

"What happened, Becca?" he asked, clomping up the wooden steps with a kitten latched onto one of his crutches. "You got pregnant. What did the bastard do, leave you?"

She rang the doorbell. Her words were quiet, but they delivered all the sting of a slap. "You found that easy enough to do."

Self-loathing lashed out like a whip inside him. She was right, but he wanted to believe he would have done the right thing by her had he known. "Rebecca, if you were pregnant, if you'd told me—"

"What?" she asked on a half-laugh, more than willing to let him squirm. "You might have sent me your forwarding address? Or maybe I would have rated season tickets to all the Kings' home games?"

The door swung open, and Muriel Marquardt squinted up at them, merry brown eyes twinkling behind a pair of rhinestone-studded glasses. She was all of five feet nothing and had the build of the Pillsbury Doughboy. With her blue-tinted hair and cotton print apron, she was the image of the All-American grandmother.

"Ooooh, Rebecca, how nice to see you!" she exclaimed in a piping little voice. She scooped a fat gray cat off the hall table to her right and cradled the pewter-colored feline in her arms like a baby, absently stroking its white belly with a dimpled hand.

"Hi, Muriel!" Rebecca shouted. "I've brought your new boarder."

"You bought a new four-door? But I liked that little car you had. It was so cute. What did you buy, a sports car? I've always pictured you in one of those foreign jobs with the top down."

Rebecca shook her head. "No. I've brought the man who's renting a room from you."

"Jace Cooper, Mrs. Marquardt," Jace shouted. He offered her his hand. Her cat reached out a paw and batted it at him.

"Mr. Cooper!" Muriel's face lit up even more in recognition. She cuddled her cat to her ample bosom. "Don't mind Chester. He's such a card. Justin and his little friends have been trying to teach him the high five. Come in, come in."

She shuffled back from the door and started down the wide hall. A trio of calico cats hopped out from behind a dilapidated potted palm to follow her. At the sight of the strangers, two of them scooted under a library table.

The house was as imposing on the inside as it was on the outside. Barely a drop of the fading sunlight penetrated the ancient brocade drapes. Dark, ornately carved woodwork dominated the walls and added to the gloom. The furniture looked sturdy enough for elephants to stand on.

"You know," Muriel mused aloud, "I hadn't given much thought to renting, but I think it just might work out. This old house has been so empty since my Winston passed on."

"Her husband passed away about a year ago," Rebecca explained as they followed the woman down the hall, passing a large, dust-covered electric organ. "She's more or less shut herself up in this house ever since."

"Without ever opening a window," Jace muttered, making a face. The aroma that hung in the air was one unique to musty old houses filled with cats.

"Frankly, I'm surprised anyone was able to talk her into renting a room. Who—"

"What's she like?" Jace interrupted as they continued toward the back of the house.

"Oh, she's sweet, a little absent-minded and hard of hearing."

"No kidding," he said dryly. "Does she like cats?"

"Here you go, Mr. Cooper," Muriel said, standing to one side of the doorway. As she swept her arm in invitation, Chester did a back flip to the floor. "I decided you might as well have two rooms since I have plenty more to roam around in. There's a bathroom just down the hall, and the back porch is right out through that door."

Rebecca passed through the small sitting room to the bedroom and dropped Jace's bag on the sturdy mahogany-framed bed. Definitely not Jace's style, she thought as she glanced around at the heavy green drapes and the antique fringed lampshades. The place looked like a funeral parlor from a Vincent Price movie.

Back in the sitting room, Chester had taken a place on a burgundy fainting couch and lay sprawled on his belly, glaring at Jace with unblinking yellow eyes. Jace had backed up to the window and was trying to raise it as he spoke.

"This is fine, Mrs. Marquardt. Very nice."

"You don't smoke, do you, Mr. Cooper? I can't stand smoking. It stinks a place up so."

"No, ma'am, I don't smoke." As he turned he bumped his bad leg against a low table and winced.

Rebecca leveled a no-nonsense look at him and pointed to the next room. "To bed. Now."

Jace grinned and winked at Mrs. Marquardt. "Now there's an offer I can't refuse."

Muriel's eyes rounded in shock like bright little marbles. "Rebecca! You young ladies nowadays are too assertive. There'll be no hanky-panky here."

"Jace is a patient of mine," Rebecca explained.

Blue-tinted curls bounced as the landlady shook her head. "Well, there'll be no playing doctor in my house."

"You don't understand. He just had knee surgery. He should be lying down."

"Oh. Fine." Her face brightened with understanding, and she smiled like a cherub. "Just so you're not with him, dear."

Rebecca shot Jace a glare as he settled on the chenille spread with his back against the headboard and patted the spot beside him invitingly. To Muriel she said, "There's no danger of that."

She helped Jace ease a pillow beneath his knee and gently loosened the Velcro-ended straps that held the brace tight. "Muriel, do you have any ice?"

"Mice? With all these cats around? Heavens no! Why, I can't remember the last time I saw a mouse."

"No, no. *I—C—E.* For Mr. Cooper's leg."

"Oh! Why didn't you say so?" Muriel scurried out with Chester at her heels.

"When did you quit smoking?" Rebecca asked. She had pleaded with him endlessly the summer of their romance to give up the habit. Jace had seemed certain he was somehow immune to the adverse effects. "That should have made the national news under 'Believe It or Not.' "

"It's part of the new me."

"So far I don't like the new you much better than the old you."

"You will, Becca," he said softly. "I promise you will."

She dodged his earnest blue gaze. The tensions of the day were ganging up to renew the pounding headache she'd had earlier. The last thing she needed to hear was another version of Jace's pledge to hound her. "That's no promise, that's a threat."

"Whatever you want to call it, I intend to make good on it."

Rebecca didn't comment, turning her attention solely to his knee. "Fifteen minutes with the ice, then you can go to a warm compress," she said, carefully examining the freshly scarred joint. "I don't like to see this much swelling. If it hasn't gone down sufficiently by morning, we may have to have Dr. Cornish aspirate the fluid accumulation."

At the thought of having a needle become intimate with his much-abused knee, Jace's face drained of all color until it matched the silvery ends of his hair. "Don't tease, Becca. You wouldn't really have him do that to me, would you?"

She gave him a cold, hard look. "As much as I would love sticking you with a few needles myself, I would not instruct a doctor to do so unless it was strictly necessary to your treatment. I resent the implication that I would take advantage of my professional position to get revenge on you for our personal relationship."

"At least you're admitting we have a personal relationship."

"I have to go," she said, backing away from his bed. "Dad and Justin are waiting supper for me."

"Becca." Jace reached out and caught her wrist before she could get away. Her pulse bucked and jumped under his fingertips. "I appreciate your help. I didn't mean to imply you'd be anything less than professional; you're too damn good at your job. It's just that I'm scared spitless of needles."

Saying the word made him cringe and shiver. During his stay in the hospital following the accident and then following his knee surgery, he'd been poked with enough metal to qualify him as a human pincushion.

"Don't be mad at me," he said softly.

His voice was like cool silk on her raw feelings, but Rebecca didn't welcome the sensation.

"I'm not mad at you," she murmured. She tried to

extract her hand from the warmth of his. His expression was sweet enough to turn around the most sour disposition. It scared her that she had to keep reminding herself not to trust him. "I told you before, I don't feel anything for you."

Jace tightened his hold on her wrist. "And I told you before, I don't believe you."

"What do I have to do to make you believe me so you'll leave me alone?" she asked, hoping against hope that there would be some simple, definitive test she could pass with flying colors. However, she wasn't the least prepared for the test he offered.

"Kiss me." The two words rang with challenge, and beneath the challenge ran a smoky layer of desire. Beneath desire lay memories.

Instantly Rebecca's gaze dropped to his mouth. Her heart thudded as Jace tugged her closer.

"Kiss me, and then tell me you don't feel anything, Becca."

What choice did she have? If she walked away, he would take it as a sign to go ahead with his pursuit of her. And if she kissed him . . . she swallowed hard.

Really, she told herself, there was no reason she shouldn't be able to do exactly as he instructed. She didn't want Jace Cooper in her life. This was the perfect opportunity to prove that to him.

Ignoring the sense of impending doom that weighed down on her chest, Rebecca sank to the bed. Her hip brushed his as she leaned toward him. Jace speared his fingers through her ebony hair and angled her head as he lowered his.

At the first brush of his lips across hers, she was lost. Sensation swallowed her up. New sensations and memories twined around her like silken ribbons, pulling her away from her cold resolve and binding her to a deeper truth—no man had ever made her feel the way Jace did.

His mouth was like liquid heat on hers. With lips and tongue he caressed, seduced, coaxed, and demanded. And she responded. Desire breached control like smoke would slide through the bars of a prison cell. She couldn't hold it back. She couldn't stop her trembling hands from reaching up to touch the hard planes of his whisker-roughened cheeks, couldn't stop the soft moan that floated up from the depths of her soul.

Jace banded one arm around her shoulders and pulled her closer, until she was half-lying across his lap. Her swelling breasts nestled into the hardness of his chest, her hip pressed against the hardness of his manhood. Their bodies greeted each other as if the time apart had bred nothing but hunger inside them. Rebecca suddenly felt as if her body were nothing more than a shell built to encompass the sharp ache of need, a need only Jace could satisfy.

Tears flooded her eyes as despair washed away all other emotion. How could she still want him? After the way he'd hurt her, after the way he'd simply left, how could she feel this kind of need? After all the nights she'd cried herself to sleep, how could her heart betray her so?

In one fluid movement, Rebecca broke the kiss, stood up, and started for the door.

Jace's heart was pounding. Desire throbbed through his whole body. Desire and surprise. The intensity of the kiss, of the need it had triggered, had knocked him for a loop. True, he had wanted to kiss Rebecca practically from the moment he'd seen her earlier in the day. He had actually fantasized about kissing her when he'd been lying in a hospital bed in Chicago. Renewing a relationship with her had seemed important, but he hadn't realized until now just how important.

He was in love with her.

The idea that she was leaving when he'd just made this monumental discovery didn't appeal to him in the least. He wanted to get up and go after her, but the pain in his knee prevented him.

"Becca?" he called, feeling helpless at the knowledge that she wouldn't come back this time.

He couldn't stop her, and a part of him couldn't blame her. He'd hurt her before, and she probably figured the odds were even he'd do it again.

The kiss had probably been a mistake, but he couldn't regret it. It had shaken them both right down to their socks. It had brought to light the fact that what had been between them before hadn't died. Sooner or later Rebecca was going to have to accept that.

The sooner the better, he thought as his body geared down from desire to aching frustration.

"I have to go," she whispered, not trusting her voice, not trusting herself to turn and face him.

Mrs. Marquardt passed her in the doorway. "Bye-bye, Rebecca. Say hello to your father for me." Brandishing a huge red plaid ice bag, she bustled toward Jace. "Just what the doctor ordered, Mr. Cooper."

She'd never failed a test in her life.

"You got a big, flaming F on this one, Rebecca," she muttered under her breath as she shooed an orange tabby away from her car door.

Her hands were shaking when she went to start the car. To steady herself, she sat back and took a slow, deep breath. Her head was filled with the subtle scent of Jace Cooper—warm, masculine. His taste lingered on her lips—warm, masculine—not unwanted, as her body had so rudely informed her, but unwelcome.

Swearing, she gunned the car's engine. Cats flew out from under the Honda and bounded for Muriel's sagging porch.

Dammit, she didn't want Jace Cooper back. Maybe her hormones had gone into rebellion for a wild moment or two, but she damn well did not want Jace Cooper back. She had the kind of quiet, orderly life every normal person wanted; she didn't need a human tornado like Jace to roar through and wreak havoc. She knew from experience the kind of destruction he left behind when he sailed out of town.

And he would sail out of town. He'd as much as told her he was just biding his time, waiting for the Kings to figure out they couldn't get along without him. He would leave, just as he had before. Only this time he wouldn't be dragging her heart along with him when he went. She would make certain of that.

As she turned the corner, Rebecca couldn't quite shake the mental image of the sincerity in Jace's eyes when he'd told her he had changed, that he wasn't the same man who'd broken her heart seven years before. She couldn't shake the image, but she couldn't make herself believe in it either.

Jace had been in a bad accident, and it had scared him. It was natural for people to come away from an experience like that with promises to change the way they lived their lives. That didn't mean he would keep the promise. She was certain he wouldn't.

In a way she had envied him. Jace had been brash and reckless, with little regard for the rules of polite society. He had been above the rules. A wealth of talent had made him exempt, while it had made her a prisoner of sorts.

She had always been the one to toe the line, the "good" Bradshaw girl. The pressure to accept responsibility, to live up to other people's expectations, had been with Rebecca as long as she could remember. And she had always conformed. Jace Cooper hadn't known the meaning of the word.

He hadn't changed, Rebecca thought, shaking her head.

Same old Jace.

But Rebecca knew the real danger wasn't the bad points of the old Jace. There wouldn't have been anything difficult in loathing a man who partied too hard, gambled too much, and used his friends. The real danger was her memories of the qualities that had made her fall in love with him.

Jace could be sweet and genuinely caring when it suited him. He could be a compassionate confidant. He could be insightful. He could be tender. He had understood her as no one else ever had.

Rebecca groaned as she parked the car in her garage and killed the engine. She didn't have an ounce of energy left. The only thing that had kept her going for the last few minutes had been tension, and it seeped out of her now. Her shoulders sagged. She gave in to the urge to rest her head on the steering wheel.

How was she going to be able to face Jace in the therapy room first thing in the morning? Like a predator scenting weakness in its victim, he would move in for the kill after that fiasco in his room.

She was going to have to lay down the law right away. Jace would find out in short order that she was the boss—of her therapy department and of her heart. She didn't take guff and she didn't date patients, and that was that. Rules were rules.

As if rules had ever stopped Jace Cooper.

Muttering, Rebecca scooped up her coat and purse and trudged to the back door. When she tried the knob, it was locked. A yellow light blinked at her from the control panel beside the door. The voice that spoke from the box was her own.

"I'm sorry. You can't go in. This door is security checked. At the tone you will have sixty seconds to use your house key before the alarm sounds."

As the tone sounded, she dropped her keys and then spilled the contents of her purse onto the step when she bent to retrieve them. Change scattered. Lipsticks and tampons rolled off in every direction.

"Fifty seconds," the box said in a pleasant tone.

Rebecca dropped to her knees, digging through the rubble for the house key. She pulled it up and jammed it into the lock, but still the knob wouldn't turn.

"Forty seconds."

"Oh, shut up." She rattled the knob and hit the key with the heel of her hand, all to no avail.

"Thirty seconds."

Reflecting on the lesser points of living with a retired computer science professor turned-inventor, she quickly picked up her things and walked around the side of the house to the dining room window. The table was set, ready and waiting for dinner to begin. Hugh Bradshaw occupied his usual chair. Rebecca scowled at the headline of the sports section he was reading. SUPER COOPER SENT DOWN TO MAVERICKS.

"Dad!" she yelled.

Hugh glanced up and looked around. "Daughter, what are you doing out there?"

"The door won't let me in. It's that crazy alarm system."

He shook his head. "Don't go blaming my alarm system just because you're not mechanical."

"I shouldn't have to be mechanical to get into my own house," she pointed out irritably. "Will you let me in before that thing summons the Marines or whatever it does at the end of sixty seconds?"

"The alarm was disconnected," Hugh said, swinging the back door open moments later. "I was just testing the timing mechanism." He pulled her key out of the lock and held it up. "Why didn't you use this?"

"Because it wouldn't work." She gritted her teeth at

the shake of his head. His expression clearly bemoaned her lack of mechanical ability.

Rebecca strode past him and dumped the armload of stuff that had fallen out of her purse onto the kitchen table.

"I hear Jace Cooper is back in town," Hugh said in his quiet, matter-of-fact voice.

"Yes. Do we have any mega-strength aspirin?"

Her father scratched the back of his head with one hand and propped the other at the waistband of his jeans as he watched her hunt through the cupboard. He was a trim, wiry man, two inches shorter than his eldest daughter. Age hadn't lessened his ability to read her every mood. "I take it you're not pleased."

"An understatement, to say the very least. I'm not pleased to have him in Mishawaka. I'm not pleased to have him as a patient in my PT department. And I'm extremely displeased to have him living across the alley from me." She washed the aspirin down with a gulp of tap water. Her thick black brows drew together in confusion. "Don't you think it's odd Muriel rented a room to him? She never mentioned wanting to do that."

Hugh mumbled something unintelligible as he bent to pull a casserole out of the oven. His thin cheeks were rosy with heat when he stood up, and his blue eyes were glued to the steam rising from the Stroganoff.

He pulled a long-handled spoon out of a crock on the counter and sank it into the fragrant mass of noodles and beef. "Who knows what Muriel thinks anymore, locked up in that mausoleum with all those cats. She needs something to get her blood going. Maybe Jace will be good for her."

"I guess it would be nice if he were good for somebody," Rebecca remarked dryly.

"But not you?"

She shook her head. "Not anymore, Dad. Not again. He wasn't any good for me before."

"That's not quite how I remember it. As I recall, you were in love with him."

"Was—past tense. I learned my lesson."

"Maybe too well," he muttered, his mustache drooping as he carried their dinner out to the table.

Rebecca stared at the back of his white head as he walked away from her. Just what had he meant by that? Somehow she didn't think she wanted to know, not at the moment at least. All she wanted was supper, a hot bath, and to get to bed early.

The image of herself and Jace sprawled on the mattress of that mahogany monster of a bed burned through her mind. Her soft mouth turned down in disapproval as she took her place at the dinner table.

Justin said grace, throwing in his request for a dog at the end. Rebecca gave him a look of reproach as she dished up his plate.

It wasn't difficult for her to steer the conversation away from Jace during dinner. Gregarious and outgoing, Justin always had a wealth of stories to relate at the end of the day.

Her father was less cooperative, but he let the subject die when she asked him about his latest project. Since he'd retired from teaching, he had spent much of his time in the basement working on computer-controlled security systems and household gadgets.

His interest in inventing had surfaced years ago, Rebecca remembered, when ALS had been steadily eroding her mother's physical abilities. He had come up with little mechanical wizards to make Gabrielle's life easier or simply to bring a smile to her lovely face. Now he worked on his inventions for enjoyment and to keep his tack-sharp mind active.

His newest project was a robot. The programming was going well, he informed her, but there were mechanical bugs to be worked out yet.

"Jace was always good with his hands," Hugh reflected. "Mechanically speaking, that is. Maybe I'll give him a call since he's going to have some free time."

Rebecca shot him a look that clearly branded him a traitor.

"You're too hard on the boy."

"The operative word there being 'boy,' as in 'has yet to grow up,' " she said.

Her father leaned his elbows on the table and pinned her with the stern gaze that had made more than one Notre Dame student squirm in his seat over the years. "You're too hard on people in general, daughter, yourself included. What happened with you and Jace happened long ago. You were both little more than kids. Don't you think it's time to forgive and forget?"

She had worked hard to forget. Until today she would have said she had forgotten. But it seemed she hadn't let go of the memory, she had simply buried it.

As for forgiveness, that was something that had never come easily to her. Life had rules. People were supposed to follow them. It had always seemed simple to her. Jace had broken the rules. She had loved him with all her young girl's heart. He had taken her heart and broken it. How could she forgive him? Why should she?

These questions haunted her all evening, through Justin's bath and bedtime right up to her own. The questions turned over and around in her brain until she became impatient with the whole process.

Dressed in her prim cotton nightgown and her reading glasses, she grabbed a pad of paper and a pen off her writing desk and settled herself in bed. With bold strokes of the pen, she made a list of the things that were bothering her, which eventually boiled down to two words: Jace Cooper. Next she made a list of her options in dealing with the problem, then eliminated the ones that didn't appeal to her.

The idea that was left on the page was the one that made the most sense: Put the past behind you and treat Jace Cooper as you would treat any other patient or acquaintance. You don't want to get involved, so don't get involved.

She congratulated herself. This was simple, this was logical, this was the intelligent way to deal with the situation. Setting her glasses and the tablet on the night table, she turned out the light and pulled the covers up around her.

Through her lace-framed window she could see across the alley to the back side of Muriel Marquardt's house. A single light burned in the window of one downstairs room near the back porch.

In the dark, with her logical pad and pen out of sight, Rebecca couldn't stop herself from wondering what Jace was still doing up. Was he in pain? Was he lonely? Was he thinking about her?

She pulled the covers up tighter around her chin, shook her head, and thought of Yogi Berra, who once had said, in a moment of profound wisdom, "It ain't over till it's over."

Four

Dawn came on the heels of a long, sleepless night. Rebecca dragged herself out of bed and went through her morning routine. It soon became obvious that it was going to be one of those days when none of her clothes fit right or combined to make an outfit and her hair defied styling. She finally gave up, put on a simple black dress, and slicked her hair back into a ponytail.

She grimaced at her reflection in the mirror above her dresser. Her skin was pale, and dark shadows lay under her green eyes. Lipstick only emphasized the drooping corners of her mouth. She felt as blue as the walls reflected in the mirror.

"You look as if you're going to a funeral," she said, "as the guest of honor."

She shrugged, then turned and left the room. The look was appropriate to her mood; why change it?

"Who died?" Hugh asked calmly as Rebecca stepped into the kitchen, made a beeline for the coffee maker, and poured herself a cup.

She shot her father a dangerous look.

"Eggs?" he asked innocently, pointing his spatula at the frying pan on the stove in front of him.

"No, thank you. I'll just have coffee this morning."

Justin stomped into the room with an ominous scowl on his usually cheerful face. He stopped in front of Rebecca, planted his hands at the waistband of his jeans, and tapped his sneaker impatiently against the linoleum. "How come I have to eat eggs and you don't?"

"Because I'm bigger than you are," Rebecca said.

The three of them sat down at the kitchen table to begin what promised to be an unpleasant meal. Justin promptly spilled a glass of milk all over himself and the floor.

"Oh, Justin!" Rebecca wailed, leaping up from her chair to grab a towel. "Now you're going to have to change clothes. You're going to be late for school, I'm going to be late for work."

He looked down at her as she sopped milk up off the floor. Sullenly he muttered, "If we had a dog, it could lick it up."

Rebecca shook a finger at him. "Don't start with that dog business, Justin. I'm in no mood."

"Yes, you are," he grumbled, tearing his toast into ragged pieces. "You're in a bad mood."

"Go change." She enunciated each word carefully.

He slid down off his chair in slow motion, tempting fate as only a small boy can. "Mom, can I go see Mr. Cooper after school?"

Rebecca's heart thudded into her breastbone. She wanted Justin and Jace together about as much as she wanted to contract malaria. Without looking up she gave her answer in a tone of voice that did not invite debate. "No."

Justin's expression clearly branded her as the most unfair mother on the face of the earth, possibly in the universe. "But Grandpa told me he's a big baseball star, and he's famous and everything!"

She rose and turned away, tossing the wet towel into the sink. "That doesn't give you the right to bother him."

"I promise I won't bother him."

"No."

"But, Mom—"

"Justin," Rebecca said sharply, wheeling to glare at him with her most dire look, "go change your clothes. I don't want to hear another word about Jace Cooper."

"Hmmm. . . ." Hugh sighed, rattling his newspaper. His mustache drooped around his mouth as he watched his grandson stomp out of the room.

"Don't start, Dad. Don't start with me," Rebecca said.

"Did I say anything?"

"Yes. You said 'Hmmm,' " she accused. Plopping down onto her chair, she crossed her arms over her chest.

He rolled his eyes and calmly turned back to his paper. "Seems a fella can't do much of anything around here without getting your back up."

"My back isn't up." She sniffed indignantly, deliberately slouching on her chair.

"Then why jump all over Justin just because he wants to meet Jace? It's only natural for a boy to want to get to know a sports star."

"I don't want him hanging around with Jace."

"And why is that?"

Because if Justin spent time with Jace, that would mean she would inevitably end up spending time with Jace, and that was the very thing that had kept Rebecca tossing and turning as night had faded into morning. After the way her body had responded to his kiss, she didn't trust herself to go anywhere near him outside the physical therapy department.

"Because he's a bad influence," she said when she realized her father was waiting for an answer.

"Oh, I see." He chewed thoughtfully on fluffy scrambled eggs and washed them down with a swallow of orange juice. "You're afraid Justin will start doing unnatural things such as playing baseball."

"That's not what I mean, and you know it."

Hugh put his fork down across his stoneware plate and rested his elbows on the table. "Daughter, you're making Jace sound like a child molester. As I remember, he's very good with kids. He used to help out with Little League. The kids loved him."

"You're making him sound like a father figure."

"Hmmm . . ."

"There you go again with that 'Hmmm' business," she said, more rattled by her fleeting thought of Jace as a father than by her own father's mutterings. "It seems to me you have a very convenient memory where Jace Cooper is concerned," she said. "You only remember his good points."

"And you only remember his bad points," Hugh retorted, then buried his nose in the entertainment section.

"They live on in infamy," Rebecca grumbled, taking a sip of lukewarm coffee.

In fact, she was ready to add to Jace's list of faults. He made her lose sleep, fight with her family, and drink cold coffee. He kissed her until she wasn't sure who she was or what she wanted. He butted into her life when everything was sailing along smoothly. The man was an utter cad.

And he was going to be waiting for her when she got to work, she realized as she glanced at her watch.

What a rotten day. And it wasn't even eight o'clock yet.

•　•　•

Jace was holding court when Rebecca walked into the exercise room. He sat on a table surrounded by an assortment of patients, doctors, and nurses. He may have faded out of the spotlight in Chicago, but in Mishawaka he was definitely hot property.

"You look as if you could use this," Dominique said, pressing a cup of coffee into Rebecca's hand.

Rebecca stared morosely across the room. The small crowd around Jace burst into laughter at something he'd said. It should have been illegal for someone so irresponsible to wield so much charm. "I could submerge myself in a vat of coffee, but I still don't think it would help."

"Didn't get much sleep because you were worried about seeing him in here today, huh?"

Rebecca glanced up at her friend with a rueful expression. "I didn't get much sleep knowing he had just moved in with my neighbor across the alley."

Dominique smoothed a hand down the purple knit dress that hugged her heart-stopping figure. "Hmmm . . ."

Rebecca sighed. "Oh, please, not you, too, Dominique."

"What did I say?"

Rebecca rolled her eyes and let the subject drop. The group surrounding Jace erupted into another round of raucous laughter. Dr. Cornish looked as if he might faint from lack of oxygen. A shapely blond nurse from orthopedics leaned close to Jace and patted his shoulder affectionately as she giggled.

Tossing back her coffee, Rebecca crumpled the Styrofoam cup and flung it into the trash, then crossed the room with a purposeful stride. She stopped short of the circle of admirers and planted her hands on her hips.

"The fascinating story of the misadventures of Super Cooper will have to continue at a later time, people. I, for one, have work to do," she said in a tone so sharp it could have carved stone.

At the sound of her voice the crowd parted like the Red Sea. They dispersed after one glance at the look on Rebecca's face. She heard them leaving, but she didn't turn to watch them go. Her gaze was unwillingly riveted to Jace. He sat on the table, his legs dangling over the edge, with a hand braced on either side of him and his navy blue eyes staring steadily at her. Heat spread under the surface of her skin like wildfire as her body recalled their last encounter.

" 'Morning, Becca," he said softly. "Did you sleep well?"

"Perfectly," she lied.

Jace considered calling her on it, but decided against it. She looked angry enough already. "I didn't," he admitted.

"Was your knee bothering you?"

"Some. My conscience was bothering me more," he said honestly. "I'm sorry I pushed so hard yesterday, Becca."

Dammit, Rebecca thought, he was doing it again. He was throwing her completely off balance. The Jace she remembered didn't make apologies for his behavior, no matter how outrageous. She had been set to lay into him tooth and nail for disrupting her department. Now he'd taken the wind out of her sails with a few softly spoken words.

Well, she thought, suddenly melancholy with remembrance, his voice had always been able to do strange things to her. When he spoke in that soft, intimate way, it was as if his voice were weaving a sensual web around her brain, effectively cutting off her highly efficient thought process.

Entranced, she stared at the clear lines of his mouth,

the neat archer's bow shape of his upper lip, and the tiny silver scar that angled away from it. It was amazing how this one part of his body could wrest away her control, but then this one part of his body was very versatile and talented. It could soothe her with words, sear her with kisses . . .

"I apologize for upsetting you, but I don't regret kissing you," he said.

Rebecca nearly bolted at the sound of his voice, but caught herself and stepped forward. "Stop staring at my mouth," she said half under her breath.

Jace chuckled. "Was I staring at your mouth? That's probably because I was remembering what it tastes like."

Rebecca was all too aware that they had a captive audience. Dominique was watching from the corner of her eye as she worked with Mrs. Krumhansle. Mrs. Krumhansle was even less discreet. Bob Wilkes sat at a weight machine across the room, halfheartedly lifting a dumbbell as he stared at them. She could almost hear him straining to catch a word or two of the conversation.

Jace smiled. It wasn't his media smile. It wasn't his playful smile. It was the smile he trotted out after an intimate encounter—lazy, disgustingly knowing. When he spoke, his voice was as warm and soft as flannel sheets. "What were you thinking about while *you* were staring at *my* mouth?"

"That's it." Rebecca bit the words off. She swung her arm toward her door. "Into my office. Now."

"Gee, honey," he teased, "can't you wait until we get home?"

She thrust his crutches at him and stormed toward the office, barely resisting the urge to kick the door in. Jace followed, wincing—not at any pain in his knee, but at the thought of the tongue-lashing he was obviously going to get.

"I won't stand for it, Jace," Rebecca said as soon as the door clicked shut behind him. "I will not have you undermining my authority in this department. I agreed to work with you to rehabilitate your knee. The least you can do is respect my position here."

"I do."

"Oh, really?" she asked, pacing back and forth behind her desk.

"Yes," he said evenly. "I have all the respect in the world for your position here, Becca. I don't think a little teasing is going to undermine your authority. Don't your other patients tease you a little every once in a while?"

They did, but the big difference was, she didn't have a past with any of her other patients. Their sometimes ribald comments meant nothing to her, they were sheer bravado. Jace's were sheer torture.

"It's your entire attitude that bothers me, Jace," she said, calling on the vast reserves of anger she had stored up against him. The only thing that made any sense to her in this situation was keeping him at least an arm's length away. "I won't have you turning my therapy department into a three-ring circus. You came here to work, not to hold fan club meetings."

"Hey, I didn't invite those people in here," he said, lifting his hands innocently.

"Tell me you weren't enjoying the attention," Rebecca said sarcastically.

"I'm a minor celebrity. It goes with the territory. What was I supposed to do? Shoot them? Ward them off with a rope of garlic? Maybe I should have come in incognito." His eyes twinkled with sudden mischief. "I could have worn my Tommy Lasorda costume."

The ludicrous image made the corners of Rebecca's mouth quirk. She clearly remembered the costume party

Jace had dragged her to seven years before. She had ended up having the time of her life. Naturally, Jace had stolen the show with his impersonation of the well-known Dodger manager. Now Rebecca pressed a fist to her lips to keep from laughing.

It must have been the lack of sleep, she thought. She was suddenly feeling giddy instead of angry. Naturally she didn't want to consider the possibility that her weird state of mind had anything to do with being alone in a room with Jace. She didn't want to think he could disarm her so easily.

"Just a minor celebrity, huh?" she questioned. "Are you always so modest?"

"No." He chuckled, picking up her paperweight and tossing it from hand to hand. "Are you always so pleasant to your patients first thing in the morning?"

"No." Her green eyes glittered like peridots. "Sometimes I get PMS."

For a moment they laughed together like old friends, and Jace took hope. Rebecca's wounds were still tender, but they hadn't totally scarred her heart. She could still laugh with him. She would love with him again in time, if he were lucky and careful. It was going to take just the right combination of pushing and coaxing and convincing her he had changed. He felt as if he were walking a tightrope over a mine field, but the reward at the end of the line was going to be worth it.

He'd spent half the night picturing them as a family—himself and Becca and Justin. Justin. He made a mental note to call his mother and ask her if he'd had freckles when he was six.

"Maybe we should start the day over," he suggested. Immediately he thought of the way he would have liked the day to have started—with Becca in his arms. It had been pure masochism to lay in bed remembering what it was like to have her there beside him, to wake up with her cuddled against him. With an effort he pushed the image away.

It was a safe bet Becca hadn't slept any better than he had. Of course, he'd given up betting, but the fact remained that there were shadows under her eyes and her temper was obviously on a short leash. He'd seen the light burning in her bedroom window until past midnight.

"Truce?" he asked.

For a long moment Rebecca stood considering the possibilities. Maybe if they declared a truce, the war inside her would stop raging as well. She could still keep her distance from him, and she wouldn't constantly be wearing herself out with anger. She thought of the list she'd made of ways to handle the situation with Jace. Hadn't her solution essentially been a truce? She had told herself to treat him as she would any old acquaintance and put the past behind her.

"Truce," she said, nodding. "But you have to understand the ground rules, Jace. This is my ballpark, I'm the manager and the head umpire. It's essential that I maintain a certain level of control. Do you understand?"

He understood. She was telling him to keep his distance. He nodded but reserved comment. Understanding and agreeing with her were two different things.

"Good," she said. "Let's go take a look at that knee."

"Becca?" he asked as she reached for the doorknob.

"What?"

Jace shook his head and smiled engagingly. "You're much too pretty to be an umpire."

If Rebecca had thought all her problems were over just because Jace had agreed to behave himself, she soon found out she was mistaken. Jace sat on the examination table in a pair of navy blue running shorts, his muscular legs magnificently bare. Somehow she had managed not to think about the fact that she was going to have to touch him. Often.

She was going to have to put her hands on his thigh, feel the crisp hair against her palms, feel the flexing and relaxing of those muscles without remembering. If she let her guard down for one second and remembered running her hands over his thighs as they made love, she was going to be in major trouble. She was going to suffer spontaneous combustion and melt down into a puddle on the floor of the exercise room. That would more or less ruin her image as head honcho of the PT department.

She swallowed hard and went on staring at his knee, trying to school her thoughts and call upon the logic that had always ruled her brain.

"How's it look?" Jace asked nervously. "Is the swelling down enough?"

"Huh?"

"Please, Becca, tell me I'm not going to have to see any n-e-e-d-l-e-s."

"Oh!" She snapped back to the business at hand. "No, it looks much better today."

Professionalism, Rebecca, she told herself. You're a professional. Keeping the thought uppermost in her mind, she grasped Jace's leg with hands that weren't quite steady and slowly began to examine his knee. She relaxed as she performed a battery of familiar stability tests. This was her field; she knew it inside out.

"Have you been doing your isometric exercises?"

"Religiously. Am I ready to go on to weights?"

"We'll see. Are you that anxious to get out of Mishawaka?"

"No," he said, choosing his words carefully. "I'm that

anxious to get back to baseball. I want you to understand what this means to me, Becca. The Kings' management isn't counting on me coming back. In fact, they're pretty sure I won't come back. They sent me down here hoping I would take it for the slap in the face it is and retire."

"Why would they do that? I'm told you're as good a third baseman as anybody in the game."

"I've also been a pain in management's rear," he said, frowning darkly. "They aren't any more willing to believe I've changed than you are."

Rebecca examined his leg in silence as she tried to deal with her feeling of guilt. No, she wasn't willing to believe he'd changed. The fact that her attitude hurt him was evident in his tone of voice.

"I've never had to work this hard for something I want," he went on. "Maybe a couple of years ago I couldn't have done it, but I can do it now. I'll give a hundred and ten percent to prove it."

He certainly sounded sincere. As his therapist Rebecca owed it to him to believe in him. As a woman she owed it to herself to be wary of him. How was she supposed to do both?

First things first, she thought, easing his leg back down to the table. "I'll settle for a hundred percent. That extra ten percent could do more harm than good. I'll put you on what I feel is the maximum program for you, Jace. Don't exceed it. Your knee can take only so much strain."

Jace nodded as he swung his legs up onto the table and straightened them out in front of him as she instructed. "You're the boss."

"Don't you forget it." She smiled at him, grasping his thigh just above his injured knee. "Tighten this muscle for me. Tighter. Tighter. Good. Relax."

"What about dinner tonight?" he asked a bit too loudly.

Suddenly the PT room was silent. Not one machine clanged. Not one person so much as breathed. Every eye was riveted on the two of them. It was like being in an E. F. Hutton commercial.

"What about it?" Rebecca asked calmly.

"What do you feel like eating? Steak? Chinese? Italian?"

The density of the silence around them increased to deafening proportions.

She gave Jace a bland smile and congratulated herself on her brilliance. This was the moment she'd been waiting for. "Sorry, Jace. I don't date patients—ever."

Murmurs ran around the room, rising and falling like a wave.

Jace narrowed his eyes as he studied the look on Rebecca's face. She thought she'd outfoxed him. Well, he'd gotten around that rule of hers once before; he would do it again.

"Ask anybody here," Rebecca said. "They'll tell you the same thing. I don't date patients. It's a very bad idea, as I once found out."

"Times change, Becca," he said softly. "People change. Policies change."

"Not around here."

He held her gaze with his own for a few long seconds. "We'll see."

Suddenly a hand encased in a sweat sock appeared under Jace's nose. He jerked back in surprise and stared at the thing. The sock had a face painted on it—expressive brown eyes, a big nose with a little black mustache beneath it, red lips. A tuft of unraveled black yarn had been stitched on top to simulate hair.

"She doesn't date patients, Jace the Ace," the sock

said in a funny little voice. "You're out of luck, lame duck."

Jace's eyes darted from the sock to Rebecca. She was calmly looking over his shoulder at the owner of the hand puppet.

"Hello, Turk," she said.

The man stepped around the table to stand beside her. He was tall and built like a licorice whip with the facial features of a goose. A silly-looking mustache wiggled under his nose like some exotic angora caterpillar. He stood with his right arm raised so his sock hand puppet was at shoulder level.

"Jace, meet Turk Lacey—"her gaze slid meaningfully to the sock—"and Mr. Peppy."

"Nice to meet you," Jace mumbled. He started to hold his hand out, then pulled it back. Turk probably wouldn't like it if he touched Mr. Peppy. At any rate, he wasn't sure he wanted to.

"Turk," Dominique said, tapping the man on the shoulder. "I'm ready for you."

Mr. Peppy's eyebrows waggled lasciviously while Turk's gaze wandered the room innocently. "And I'm ready for you, long tall lady." The sock winked at Jace. "Catch you later, Super Cooper."

Dropping Mr. Peppy to his side, Turk turned and fell into step beside the therapist. Dominique gave a little jump and leveled a no-nonsense look at the man. "Mr. Peppy had better watch his mouth, or he's going to need darning."

Turk merely shrugged one shoulder and wiggled his mustache.

"Friend of yours?" Jace asked Rebecca.

"Teammate of yours," she said with a malicious smile. "I'm hoping he'll be your roommate on the road."

"Geez, Becca, you've developed a real sadistic streak," he said, craning his neck so he could see Turk Lacey.

Dominique was frowning prettily as she examined the man's left shoulder in a way that indicated he had a rotator cuff injury. "He plays for the Mavericks?"

"He's their ace relief pitcher."

"That explains a lot." He looked up at her. "Becca, the man talks through a hand puppet."

"Oh, you noticed that, did you?"

Bob Wilkes rolled up beside Jace's table in his wheelchair. "The guy's got a slider that'll blow your kneecaps off."

Jace cringed at the reference.

"Oh, hey, sorry, Jace," Wilkes said. He glanced up at Rebecca, then shook his head. "She really doesn't date patients, but every guy in the place will wish you luck if you want to take a shot."

"Bob," Rebecca said through her teeth, "shouldn't you be in the whirlpool—headfirst?"

He wheeled back out of her reach and winked at Jace. "She's a tigress. See ya 'round, Acer."

Jace managed to contain his mirth to a tight smile as Rebecca shot him a look. His eyes gleamed. "He's got you pegged, Becca."

"I'm amazed you didn't bet him you could get me to go out with you," she said dryly. "The odds should be irresistible to you."

"I don't gamble anymore."

Rebecca stared at him in disbelief. "Let me get this straight. You've quit smoking, you've quit gambling. Does the sun still rise in the east, or have I missed that monumental change too?"

"The sun still rises in the east," he said, his gaze as level as his voice. "You can be as sure of that as you can be of me getting a date with you."

"Then we'd better alert the scientific community, because I'm not going to start seeing you again, Jace."

She dismissed the topic as if it didn't make her pulse jump erratically and turned her attention back to his knee. "Try to raise your leg off the table against the pressure of my hand."

Jace worked diligently through a series of exercises. Rebecca recited to him the names of the seven ligaments of the knee. She explained that he had anterior cruciate ligament damage and a torn meniscus, and outlined the kind of rehabilitation program she thought would work best to get his knee in maximum working order as quickly as was medically prudent.

The odd thing about the conversation was that Jace actually listened. He didn't seem bored in the least by all her technical talk. Rebecca remembered trying to explain his shoulder separation to him. The only thing he'd been interested in was brushing his arm against her breast as she'd tested the joint for range of motion. Now he listened attentively and even interrupted her to ask questions about the amount and kind of exercise he should give the knee outside of the therapy room. He nodded as she explained the program of additional isometric exercises and light weight training he would be starting on.

Maybe, Rebecca mused, he had grown up after all.

"And how long are you going to keep feeling up my thigh?" Jace asked.

Rebecca looked down at his leg. Lord, she was doing it again! Her fingers had crawled up from his knee and were rhythmically kneading the sculpted muscle high on his thigh. Her face flushed fire engine red as she jerked back. Primly she said, "I was merely testing the tone of your quadriceps."

"Hmmm . . . do you want to test the tone of any other parts of me?" he asked just loud enough for her to hear. "I could suggest one appendage in particular that seems to be developing excellent tone."

Rebecca glared at him. So much for Jace's maturing. So much for their truce. True to form, he had made a promise, then broken it at the first opportunity. She straightened up and stepped back from him. "I think this session is about over."

Jace shrugged. "If you say so. What about that dinner date?"

"What about our truce?"

"I don't consider asking for a date subversive behavior."

She relaxed a little, more out of resignation than anything. He hadn't changed, he never would. "Fifteen minutes in the whirlpool, then you can leave."

"How about a massage?" he asked hopefully.

"Not today," Rebecca said, turning away from him, unwilling to admit she was disappointed their truce hadn't worked out the way she had hoped. It was best for her to remember he wasn't trustworthy, she told herself.

"Shirking your responsibilities, Ms. Therapist?" he teased, hoping to goad her into touching him again. She may have pretended she wanted nothing to do with him, but her fingers told their own version of the story when they made contact with his body.

Rebecca wheeled on him, unable to hold her anger completely in check. "No. That was always your department," she said cuttingly. Impatiently her gaze scanned the room. "If you really want a massage, I believe Max is free."

Jace gulped at the sight of Max, a blond behemoth who made Conan the Barbarian look like Pee-Wee Herman. "Is he any relation to the Incredible Hulk?"

"Yes," Rebecca gave him a nasty smile. "Max is his meaner brother."

"Maybe I'll pass on that massage after all. I have to get home so I can help Muriel wash windows."

"Your choice," she said, walking away.

Jace watched her go, admiring the subtle sway of her hips as she glided toward her office. He had his work cut out for him trying to win her back, but he was discovering that the new Jace Cooper found the taste of challenge sweet.

He jumped as Mr. Peppy, the animated sweat sock, made another unexpected appearance directly under his nose.

"What's the matter, Super Cooper? Did you strike out?"

Jace scowled at the hand puppet. "How would you like to get unraveled?"

Five

Rebecca sat bolt upright in bed as the strains of "Take Me Out to the Ball Game" blasted in through her open window. The organist built to an ear-splitting crescendo, then stumbled through an off-key segue into "Lady of Spain." It was quite plain the organist possessed more enthusiasm than talent. It was also quite plain the organist was nearby. Every dog in the neighborhood had begun to howl.

Struggling to get her arms into the sleeves of her robe, Rebecca shuffled across the room, bent over, and peered out the window. She combed her hair back out of her eyes. It was a beautiful Saturday morning. The sun was shining. Puffy white clouds dotted the blue sky like marshmallows. No doubt the birds had been singing until the attack of the Wurlitzer. The air was pure and sweet, and Jace Cooper was making his way across her lawn with a smile on his face.

He moved carefully, leashing the athletic grace that came to him so naturally. In jeans and a knit shirt, he was the very image of maleness. The Lenox-Hill brace was strapped firmly to his knee, as it would be for some time, but his crutches were gone.

Rebecca froze like a deer in headlights as Jace locked his gaze on her. Two weeks of dealing with him as a patient had done nothing to lessen her awareness of him as a man. If anything, she was even more aware of his body. She couldn't seem to stop thinking about the way his muscles flexed and strained beneath her hands, or the warm, smooth texture of his skin.

Nor could she stop thinking about the amount of determination he'd shown. Not once had Jace uttered a complaint about the work she'd put him through. He had even asked for her permission to make use of the weights in the PT room to keep his upper body in shape. When she'd questioned him about what had happened to all the expensive fitness equipment he had owned, he'd merely shrugged and told her he didn't have it anymore.

She wondered at her own motives for letting him hang around her department longer than was strictly necessary. At first she had told herself it was to show him how unaffected she was by his presence. That was a bad strategy. She was all thumbs and left feet when Jace was around, bumping into, tripping over, and dropping things. It was a wonder she hadn't ended up in the hospital herself. And it seemed she couldn't keep her eyes off him. He was like forbidden fruit—handsome, tempting, dangerously alluring.

Rebecca had thought perhaps Jace meant to hound her during his extra time in the exercise room. He hadn't given up on asking her out, constantly coaxing and teasing her during their therapy sessions. But he did indeed spend his extra time working or offering encouragement to other patients, and it was quite clear to Rebecca that he was doing neither to score points with her. More than once he had looked up and been genuinely surprised to see her watching him. His surprise had quickly turned to a warm, playful smile, not unlike the one he was sending her now as he made his way carefully across her lawn.

"I fixed Muriel's organ," he said proudly, stopping at the window of her first-floor room.

"So I hear." Rebecca grimaced as Muriel mistook a sharp for a flat in the Mexican hat dance song. "I wouldn't do much bragging about that around the neighborhood if I were you. You're not likely to endear yourself to many people."

Jace leaned closer to the window and gave her a look that combined seduction and sincerity in a way that made Rebecca's knees quiver. "I'm only interested in endearing myself to you."

"Then go throw a wrench into that thing," she said. "Saturday is my morning to sleep in."

As if she'd gotten a moment's sleep since Jace had moved back into her life, she thought, rubbing at eyes that felt fur-covered from lack of rest.

Jace shook his head, his silvery hair fluttering in the breeze. "No can do, honey. Muriel needs to practice."

"No kidding," she said on a groan. "Bach must be rolling over in his grave."

"I'll admit she's a little rusty, but she'll improve." His optimism was lost on Rebecca. "I got her the job as organist at the ballpark for all the Mavericks' home games. She's thrilled."

Rebecca stared at him, stunned. "You got Muriel to take a job? She's hardly left that house since Winston died. She sends out for her groceries, and you got her to take a job?"

"She needs to get out," he said simply. "People need involvement and human contact."

And Jace had cared enough to help Muriel find it. Not quite knowing what to say, Rebecca let her gaze wander across the alley to the ugly old house with the peeling brown paint. Freshly planted marigolds brightened the edge of the cracked sidewalk. Half a dozen cats sunned themselves on the back porch. Ancient brocade drapes stirred in the morning breeze. Her eyes rounded in wonder.

"She's opened the windows," she said, amazed. "She hasn't opened those windows since she accidentally set the kitchen on fire last year."

Jace met her stunned look with a sheepish one, then glanced down and started picking cat hair off his violet polo shirt. "I told her I'd read somewhere that houses should be aired regularly to prevent a buildup of radon gas."

Rebecca laughed. "I'd say the end justifies the means in this case. Having been in Muriel's house, I have to say those curtains blowing in the breeze are a lovely sight."

Jace's dark brows lifted as his gaze strayed down from her face. "The view over here isn't too bad either."

Rebecca glanced down at herself. Her robe hung open and her cotton nightgown was gaping away from her chest as she bent over, giving Jace an unobstructed view of her breasts. Gasping, she clutched the fabric to her throat in a white-knuckled fist, stood up—and smacked her head sharply on the raised window.

"Ouch! Damn you, Jace Cooper!" she said, squeezing her eyes shut against the pain. "You're going to be the death of me!"

"Are you okay?"

"No, I'm not okay," she said irritably, rubbing a hand through her disheveled hair to find the sore spot on her head.

"Should I come in and kiss it?" he asked in his most seductive voice.

Rebecca scowled at him. "I'll tell you what you can kiss, you obnoxious pain in—"

"Now, honey," Jace said in a warning tone. "Not in front of the children."

She glanced around as Justin shuffled up behind her, the feet of his astronaut pajamas scuffing along on the blue carpet. He had obviously just rolled out of bed. Ink-black hair hung down in front of sleepy blue eyes. He clutched a ragged stuffed dog to one shoulder.

"Hi, Mom. Did you hit your head again?"

Rebecca gritted her teeth at his excellent memory but knelt down to hug him just the same. He really was the sweetest thing on two legs, and she loved him to distraction. She brushed his hair out of his eyes and kissed his forehead. "Yes, sweetheart, I hit my head," she said pleasantly. "It's all Mr. Cooper's fault."

Justin peered out at Jace, curiosity waking him up even more than Muriel Marquardt's horrible organ playing. "Hi, Uncle Jace. Are you a window peeker?"

"No." Jace chuckled, wishing he could scoop the boy up and hug him. He had become very attached to Justin in the short time they'd been neighbors. The kid was a real charmer, and he looked so like Rebecca— except for his blue eyes. "Your mom and I were just having a conversation."

"If we had a dog, it would chase window peekers away, wouldn't it?"

Jace grinned and nodded. "I suppose so."

Rebecca sighed defeatedly and brushed at an errant strand of hair that had fallen across Justin's forehead. "Justin, honey, for the millionth time, we can't get a dog. If we got a dog, it would have to stay in the house, and I'd break out in a terrible rash and my face would puff up and my nose would stuff up and my eyes would water and I'd be miserable. You wouldn't want that, would you?"

The boy stood considering for a moment, his black brows pulled low over his eyes and a frown tugging down the freckles on his cheeks. He hugged his toy a little harder and looked down at the floor. "I guess not," he mumbled dejectedly.

Justin had loved dogs since he'd been a toddler. It just about broke Rebecca's heart to deny him. One of his first words had been "puppy." She tried to remind herself that an allergy didn't make her a terrible mother. The thought evoked another memory: one of her sister bitterly telling her she would be a perfect mother, since she was perfect at everything else. She bit her lip at the sharp pain of remembrance.

"Justin," Jace said, his gaze on Rebecca's suddenly strained expression. She was as white as the painted woodwork of her room. "Go see if Grandpa has the pancakes started, okay?"

When the boy was out of the room, Jace leaned his forearms against the screen. "Becca?" he asked softly. He wished he were inside so he could scoop her up and hug her. She looked as if she needed someone to lean on. He was determined to be that someone. He was really going to have to do something about this living-in-the-wrong-house business—the sooner the better. "Honey, are you all right?"

"I'm fine," Rebecca said around the knot in her throat.

"When did you take up lying?"

When you came back, she thought. His reappearance in her life had forced her to take up a host of vices: Lying, denying needs, denying emotions. She wondered if he had any idea of the Pandora's box he'd opened up inside her.

"You're terrible at it," Jace said with affection rather than censure.

"Thanks."

"Don't mention it." Once again his voice took on that

soothing quality that made Rebecca want to wrap herself in it. "Becca, it's me, remember? Nobody knows you the way I do. You can tell me anything."

And then you'll walk away and break my heart, she thought. Misery throbbed inside her. "Can I tell you to leave?"

"Sure," he said affably, "but I won't go."

"Why not?"

"Because I love you."

Her heart gave a great thud at his admission. She had to lean against the windowsill as a combination of weakness and dizziness swirled through her.

"Besides," Jace said, pushing himself back from the window, "your dad invited me to breakfast."

Rebecca gaped at him as he limped toward the back door. How could he just say something like that and then calmly walk away? Wasn't that just like him, she thought, suddenly furious. He'd probably said it only for shock value.

As if he'd read her mind, Jace turned at the door. "I mean it, Becca," he said, dead serious. "Straight from the heart."

He punched a couple of buttons on the control panel of Hugh's security system and let himself into the house.

Hugh and Jace were discussing electronics when Rebecca finally made it into the kitchen. As she put on a pair of casual slacks and a loose cotton top, combed her hair and fussed with a tube of mascara, she told herself she was stalling in the hope that Jace would leave—and not primping so he would think she looked nice.

His profession of love had rattled her to the core. Every time she turned around, it seemed he was saying something else to rock the foundation of her opinion of him. Now this. How was she supposed to react? At another time, in a place in her past, she would have been overjoyed to hear those words from him. She *had* been overjoyed. She had accepted his love with a wonderful, youthful enthusiasm and given her own love freely in return. But it had also been Jace who had taught her how shallow love could be, how quickly other things could turn its head, how deeply it could hurt.

Wariness and anger were the emotions that surfaced most easily now. Despite his claims, she couldn't allow herself to trust him, and it angered her that he could toy with her feelings so cavalierly. Damn him, anyway. Who did he think he was, sauntering back into her life after seven years and turning it upside down?

Jace Cooper, that's who he was. But was he the Jace Cooper she'd known, or was he the man those deep blue eyes portrayed—older, wiser, changed in some deeper way she caught fleeting glimpses of from time to time?

Not wanting to think about it, Rebecca crossed the kitchen, rubbing her sore head, and opened a cupboard in search of aspirin.

Hugh glanced up at her, his white mustache twitching. "What did you hit your head on this time?"

Rebecca slanted her father a burning glare as she poured herself a cup of coffee, then pinned Jace with the same look. His eyes twinkled. "There was a Peeping Tom at my window."

Hugh frowned. "Robby Costmeyer again? I swear, that kid has a hormone imbalance."

"No," Rebecca said, still glaring at Jace. "It was some other kid with a hormone imbalance."

"This neighborhood is going to hell in a handbasket," Hugh grumbled, turning his attention back to the plans he had spread out on the table.

"I quite agree," Rebecca said as she dropped two slices of bread into the toaster.

"You're a beautiful woman, Rebecca," Jace commented, his gaze heating as he let it flow down her, from her face to her firm, full breasts, over the curve of her hip to her long legs.

She almost glanced down to make sure she had indeed put clothes on. The look he was giving her made her feel naked. But then, Jace was well aware of what she looked like undressed.

"Most men find beauty hard to resist," he said.

"Do they find a punch in the nose hard to resist?" she asked through her teeth.

She turned to the toaster and smacked it on the side. Her bread shot out like a pair of missiles. She shrieked in surprise and ducked, just missing taking a direct hit between the eyes by a piece of whole wheat. The toast arched gracefully through the air and landed on the table, right on Hugh's plans.

He shook his head while Jace bit his lip to keep from laughing. "A man couldn't ask for a better, brighter daughter, but she's a complete disaster with machines."

Rebecca snatched her toast up and leaned toward her father's ear. "Wait until you see how I am with murder weapons. I'm going to kill you for inviting him over without warning me."

The elder Bradshaw muttered something Rebecca couldn't quite catch that ended with ". . . and this is the thanks I get."

She gave him a curious look, then took her toast and coffee to the dining room, where she could eat without having to feel Jace's gaze on her—and without having to strain to keep her gaze off him, she admitted, a black mood settling over her.

The front door banged, and Justin stormed in, his face bright with excitement. "Mom, Mom! Look what

Uncle Jace gave me!" he shouted. He slowed down momentarily to hold up a fielder's glove that looked big enough to fit over his head. Seconds later he charged back out of the kitchen, his grin wide enough to show he'd lost three teeth recently. "Uncle Jace gave me this glove and a baseball with his name on it. Isn't it cool?"

It was difficult for Rebecca to share his enthusiasm. In fact, it was all she could do to keep from letting Justin see just how upset she was. It was one thing for Jace to disrupt her life—she was a big girl, she knew what to expect from him, knew his presence was only temporary—but she wouldn't have him hurting Justin, who was looking up at her with wide, trusting blue eyes.

"Uncle Jace is gonna teach me how to throw a screwball."

"Uncle Jace *is* a screwball," she murmured under her breath, rising from her chair as Jace sauntered out of the kitchen. "Oh, *Uncle Jace*," she said pointedly, "may I have a word with you?"

Jace cringed inwardly at the look in Rebecca's bright green eyes. He glanced at Justin. "Go on outside, son. I'll be right there."

Justin scampered off, oblivious to the undercurrents that were so thick the adults practically had to wade through them.

"For the last time," Rebecca said in a low voice, "he is not your son."

Jace folded his arms over his chest, settling in for the argument to come. "I don't believe you."

"I don't care what you believe." She tugged a hand through her hair and began pacing back and forth along the end of the table. "I won't have you doing this, Jace. I won't stand for it. I won't have you trying to get to me through Justin."

Jace's expression darkened at the insult. He tightened his arms against his chest to keep from reaching out and shaking Rebecca. "I'm not using Justin. When I spend time with him, it's because I enjoy being with him. He's a fabulous kid, and I have every intention of the two of us getting to know each other better."

Rebecca shook her head, feeling as if she were teetering at the very edge of her control. "I won't allow you to wrap him around your little finger until he idolizes you, and then break his heart when you leave."

The way you did to me.

The words stretched between them like a tightrope.

Jace's anger seeped out of him. Rebecca had every reason to be wary of him. He couldn't be insulted that she had such a low opinion of him when he had earned it.

He took a step closer, knowing she couldn't escape him without running around to the other side of the table—and knowing she wouldn't do that because she was too damn proud. He lifted a hand to cup her cheek. His fingertips tingled where they brushed at the teasing silkiness of her ebony hair. His thumb skimmed over her high cheekbone. "I won't hurt him, Becca. And I won't hurt you. Not this time. I promise."

"Don't make promises you know you won't keep, Jace," Rebecca said tiredly. "It only makes things worse in the end."

He dropped a quick kiss onto her mouth and stepped back before she had a chance to react. The new Jace Cooper didn't break promises, but there was no use telling Becca that. He was going to have to show her. He was determined to show her.

"I'd better get outside," he said, pointing to the front door. "Justin's waiting for me."

Rebecca frowned at him. Same old Jace. He did as he pleased, and to hell with everyone else's feelings.

He chucked her under the chin and gave her a lopsided smile. "Don't worry about Justin. We're only playing baseball."

She scowled at him. "With my luck, you'll teach him how to spit and scratch."

Saturday was traditionally the Bradshaw family's night out. Rebecca could remember them all going out together from the time she had been Justin's age—her parents and her sister and herself. They had made the rounds of family restaurants and fast food places in the South Bend–Mishawaka area. Sometimes they had followed dinner with a movie or an evening in a park or a drive into the country.

Hugh's natural affinity for teaching had turned every outing into a learning experience, and Rebecca, ever the scholar, had eagerly soaked up the information, whether it was the historical details of a building or landmark or lessons on astronomy as they gazed at the summer night sky. Ellen, who was younger by two years and not in the least interested in astronomy or anything remotely related to school, had invariably ended up getting into some kind of trouble.

When ALS had confined Rebecca's mother to a wheelchair and a rest home, their family outings had become trips to the cafeteria there or "picnics" in Gabrielle's room. The tradition had passed away with Gabrielle Bradshaw, not to be resurrected until years later.

All these memories stirred restlessly inside Rebecca as the three of them drove into the parking lot at Captain Jack's Great Fun Place. In the backseat Justin jabbered incessantly about the intricacies of playing catch with a real fielder's glove and a real ball player. Hugh kept trying to turn the conversation toward the progress he and Jace had made on his latest electronic device. Rebecca managed to nod and make monosyllabic comments at appropriate intervals. She parked her Honda next to a strangely familiar-looking black DeSoto that was at least as old as she was.

Located in an old brick warehouse, Captain Jack's was a place that boasted something for everybody. The decor was a blend of eclectic and eccentric, with everything from mounted moose heads to Studebaker hubcaps lining the walls. The restaurant section overlooked the St. Joseph River. But Captain Jack's was much more than a restaurant. There was an immense game room crammed with coin-operated rides and video games for children of all ages. Just off the game room was a dance floor where a huge, old-fashioned jukebox ablaze with neon lights stood on a raised dais.

The hostess, who was in buccaneer dress, gave Justin his complimentary King of the Pirates crown and led them toward a booth. As was usually the case on Saturday night, the place was crowded with families. The noise of people talking and eating along with the mechanical chatter of the games and the music from the jukebox combined to make a festive atmosphere. Rebecca ordered herself to shake off her melancholy mood and join in the fun.

They were more than halfway across the wood-planked floor of the dining room when she saw him—or rather, them. Jace and Muriel occupied a spacious corner booth. Rebecca's heart picked up an irregular rhythm as the unlikely couple motioned for her family to join them.

"Look, Mom, it's Uncle Jace and the cat lady!" Justin said excitedly, tugging on her hand.

"Sweetheart, please don't call Mrs. Marquardt 'the cat lady,' " Rebecca said wearily. She suddenly felt exhausted from trying to escape Jace. It was clear he meant to remain a part of her life for the duration of his stay in Mishawaka. The smart thing would have been to resign herself to that fact.

"Gee, I thought that was Muriel's old car in the parking lot," Hugh said, the surprise in his voice about as genuine as wax fruit.

Rebecca was ready to make a biting comment about his having told Jace where they were going to be for the evening, but she stopped herself. Her father had a rather unusual sparkle in his eyes as he headed for the booth. Either she was hallucinating, or that was a blush blooming on his cheeks as he said hello to Muriel Marquardt.

Her father and Muriel Marquardt?

"I'm losing my mind," she said conclusively.

"Don't be so hard on yourself, sweetheart," Jace said, taking her hand and leading her to the booth. "All you need is a good pizza."

She scowled at him. "This is not a date. If you call this a date, I'll slug you."

Jace shook his head, his blond hair tumbling into his eyes. "When did you develop this latent streak of violence?"

"When you came back to town."

He took the audacious liberty of brushing a kiss over the tender spot just in front of her right ear as he handed her into the booth. "But, sweetheart, I'm a lover, not a fighter, remember?"

Did she remember? The urge to burst into hysterical laughter was almost too much for Rebecca. She remembered every touch, every tender caress, every whispered word of passion. She'd spent every night since his return lying in bed remembering. The least provocation brought the memories so close to the surface, she trembled with renewed need.

She knew if she closed her eyes now, she would be transported to a time and place where Jace had held her in his arms and his lips had moved across her cheek in a hot trail of kisses. She would feel the tangled sheets beneath her, feel Jace's powerful body surging into her, feel the incredible buildup and climax of sensation.

"Are you all right, Rebecca dear?" Muriel asked, leaning across the table, squinting at her through rhinestone-studded glasses.

Rebecca jerked herself out of the trance she had fallen into. "Yes, yes, I'm fine, Muriel. I'm just a little tired."

Muriel's bright brown eyes widened in horror. "You've been fired? Oooh, but you're such a wonderful therapist! What is that hospital coming to?"

"Not fired, tired," Hugh shouted, leaning close to Jace's landlady.

Muriel looked up at him and breathed a sigh of relief, her dimpled hand pressed to her round bosom. "Thank heaven!" She sent Rebecca a grandmotherly smile. "All you need is to get out and have a little fun. Fun is the greatest tonic in the world. That's what Jace says."

Rebecca looked at Jace. "I'll bet," she said dryly.

She managed to make it through dinner without stringing together more than five words at a time. Between Justin's chatter about his newfound love of baseball, Hugh's excitement about his new project, and Muriel's hearing problem, Rebecca really didn't have to say much. But suddenly Hugh and Muriel were off to try their luck in the game room, and Rebecca was left with Jace and Justin, who was still in the process of finishing his dessert.

"Are you having fun?" Jace asked, his gaze holding hers in a way that somehow made escape seem impossible.

"Tons," she said morosely.

Justin grinned up at the two of them, the traces of a hot fudge sundae on his chin. "I'm having lots of fun. Captain Jack's is my favorite place."

"We'll have to come here again then, won't we?" Jace said, dabbing a napkin at the streaks of chocolate and ice cream on the boy's face.

Rebecca's heart flipped over at the tenderness of his touch and the expression in his eyes. He was truly very good with Justin. Trying to get to her through him had nothing to do with it.

Justin adjusted his pirate crown and, out of the blue, announced, "I don't have a dad."

Rebecca felt herself go pale.

Jace glanced from her back to Justin with an intense expression. How was he supposed to field a hit like that? *Very carefully, Jace old boy. This is no time for errors.* "How do you feel about that, Justin?"

Justin shrugged, rubbing a spot of chocolate off the front of his pint-sized Notre Dame T-shirt. "Sometimes it makes me sad. Most of my friends have dads. Some of their folks are divorced. I have Grandpa, though. He's cool. And now I have you, Uncle Jace. You're super cool."

He stood up on the seat of the booth and threw his arms around Jace in an unself-conscious hug. Jace hugged him back, his eyes misting over. How was it he had lived so many years without knowing what it was to want this—a wife, a home, the love of a son? Looking back, the last few years of his life seemed like such a waste of time, of talent, of everything that mattered.

"Can we go play the games now, Mom?" Justin asked brightly as he twisted around in Jace's arms.

Rebecca didn't trust herself to speak. She forced a smile and nodded. As Justin scrambled over Jace's lap, she steeled herself. Surely he would take advantage of this opportunity and bring up the subject of Justin's paternity again. She slid across the vinyl seat with her eyes lowered and glanced up in surprise when her hip bumped up against Jace's. His expression was one of concern and the same tenderness he had shown Justin.

"You're a wonderful mother, Becca," he said softly, earnestly.

Tears welled up in her eyes. He could be the sweetest man on earth. It was so unfair that he could also be the most fickle. For the moment, though, she welcomed his words and the heartfelt sentiment behind them and remembered that he had once been her best friend.

"Thank you," she whispered, trying to smile and sniffle at the same time. "I try."

"I know you do." He stroked a hand over her dark hair, which gleamed under the amber lights. In what was fast becoming a habit, Jace leaned down and kissed her softly. She offered no protest, which was encouragement enough to bring a smile to his face. "Are you ready to beat me at PacMan?"

Rebecca groaned. "You know how I am with machines."

Jace eased himself out of the booth, carefully straightening his left leg. Then he gave Rebecca a hand out. Testing his luck, he slipped an arm around her shoulders. "I'll let you cheat."

Rebecca wasn't sure who was more fun to watch, Jace and Justin or Hugh and Muriel. Her father seemed to be having the time of his life. With Muriel Marquardt. Who would have guessed, she wondered. All these years Muriel had lived right across the alley.

It made Rebecca feel a little guilty, but she had never really wondered whether her father would want another romantic involvement. He had loved Gabrielle in a way that happened once in a lifetime. It had never occurred to Rebecca that he might yearn for a relationship with another woman.

"Dad and Muriel are having a great time," she said

as Jace slid down onto a chair at the little table they had claimed off the games area.

Jace kept his eyes protectively on Justin, making sure the boy made it safely through the crowd to the machine his grandfather was playing. "Yeah. Hey, that Muriel is pretty sharp at pinball. I think she's some kind of hustler." He turned back to Rebecca with a smile that warmed her heart. "How about you, beautiful? Are you having fun?"

She smiled down at the table, embarrassed that he could still make her blush with nothing more than a look. "I'm having a very nice time."

"Gee, could you try not to sound so surprised?" he complained teasingly. "The male ego is a delicate creature."

"A delicate creature the size of a sperm whale," she corrected, chuckling. Jace reached across the table and tweaked her nose.

"Hey, look! It's Cooper!" a voice boomed above the noise of the room.

Jace looked up and grinned as two of his new teammates and their girlfriends made their way through the throng carrying pizzas and a pitcher of beer. He had begun attending team meetings, anticipating the day when he would be able to work out with the Mavericks and eventually play with them. The team was a motley crew of journeyman players, more of them on their way down than up, but they were, for the most part, nice guys. Jace had hit it off with them instantly.

"Becca," he said, standing up, "this is Pat Wylie, the Mavericks' catcher, and Jerome Tarvin, shortstop and Elvis impersonator extraordinaire."

Jerome jerked a hand back through his well-oiled pompadour, curled his lip, and sang a couple of bars of "Hound Dog." Everybody laughed and applauded. The players introduced their girlfriends and asked Rebecca how long it would be before they could get Jace into the Mavericks' lineup.

"Soon," she promised. "He's making progress."

"Not soon enough," Wylie said. "Comitzki is like a sieve at third base. Everything goes right through him. I think the guy's legally blind."

"Then he ought to give up third base and become an umpire," Jace suggested, chuckling. Jerome twisted his hips and sang a line of "Don't Be Cruel."

"It'll be a different story when we get Super Cooper in there," Pat announced as he poured mugs of foaming cold beer and passed them around the table. "Take heart! Drink up!"

Jace stared at the glass the catcher shoved in front of him. "No, thanks."

"Go ahead, Jace." Jerome laughed. "You might as well enjoy yourself before you join the ranks."

Rebecca watched Jace with curious eyes as he stared at the sweating glass. He looked like a man who was dying of thirst but had been forbidden on pain of death to take a drink. She shoved a soda into his hand and sent his friends a wry smile. "Sorry, guys, he's in training."

Jace forced a grin and shrugged. "What can I say? She's the boss."

As soon as his teammates moved on to join another group of friends, Jace suggested going out for a breath of fresh air. He didn't say a word until they reached Muriel's DeSoto, some distance away from the building. Then he leaned against the ugly monster of a car and looked up at the sky.

"Beautiful night, isn't it?"

Rebecca leaned back beside him with her hands in the pockets of her blue dirndl skirt. "You quit drinking too," she said quietly.

For once, Jace didn't come back with a snappy retort. He looked away and scuffed the sole of his Topsider against the fine gravel in Captain Jack's parking lot.

"I guess it's my turn to say we used to be friends," she said. "Whatever else has happened or will happen, you can still talk to me, Jace."

It was plain to Rebecca that she was opening a door that, to this point, she had been leaning against to keep shut. But in that instant, when Pat Wylie had pushed the drink in front of him, she had seen something in Jace, something that had convinced her he truly was trying to make changes in his life. She had seen vulnerability, fear, and the determination to not give in to it. He was a man struggling, a man who had once been her best friend in the whole world.

"I haven't had a drink in four months."

"Was it a problem?"

He laughed. "I didn't think so—until I quit."

It was kind of funny how he had thought himself to be invincible. He had partied because he liked to party, drank because he enjoyed it. There had never been a thought in his head about consequences.

That way of life had ended late one night in a tangle of metal on the Dan Ryan Expressway.

In the four months since, he had discovered what it was to *need* a drink, to crave the kind of oblivion that came from one too many. He considered it part of his punishment to deny himself that comfort. He didn't deserve to forget what had happened. He owed it to himself to remember.

"I've changed, Becca," he said, turning to look at her in the thin light of the parking lot. "I need you to believe that. I need you to believe in me."

Rebecca raised a hand to touch his cheek. Her thumb brushed across the tiny scar that angled away from his lip. She had been trying so hard to keep her distance from him, but she was discovering that some threads of an old friendship were hard to break. Looking at Jace now, she could see the changes in him. And she could see those changes had been made on a long, hard road. She had been guarding herself, concerned only about her needs in a relationship. Jace had needs, too, needs that went deeper than the physical.

Still she held back. Self-preservation was a strong instinct. She offered him what support she could. "I believe you're trying, Jace. I want you to succeed."

Knowing he had to prove himself to her, Jace tried to ignore the sting her doubt caused. At least she believed he was making the effort. He only wished she could realize what it was costing him to have to make that effort alone.

"Thanks," he whispered, bending his head to kiss her.

Rebecca went willingly into his arms. She had spent too many nights dreaming of his kiss not to. It was something they both needed for more than one reason. They needed the strength and comfort of one another's arms. They sought the sweet haze of desire to soothe old hurts and insecurities, to block out realities that were too harsh.

For this one suspended moment Rebecca let go of every thought that had plagued her logical, analytical mind and thought only of this kiss, of the taste of this man she had never forgotten. He held her so she could feel their hearts beating together. He kissed her with a hunger that bordered on desperation and yet was sweet and achingly tender.

After a long moment Jace raised his head and looked into her eyes. "Becca, I—"

"—think we'd better go back inside," she interrupted. She knew the words that were ready to tumble out of his mouth. She couldn't bear to hear them now, not when she was so dangerously close to falling in love

To get a free *Loveswept* ® calendar, packed with information about *Loveswept* romances in 1990, simply fill out the form below.

*C*alendar available early December, 1989. Offer good while supplies last.

Name _____

Address _____

City _____ State_____ Zip _____

Would you please give us the following information:

Did you buy Loveswept Golden Classics (on sale in June)?
____Yes ____No

If your answer is yes, did you buy __1 __2 __3 __4

Will you buy Golden Classics featuring Hometown Hunks on the covers?
I will buy 1-2____, 3-4 ____, All 6____ None____.

How often would you like to have an opportunity to purchase Golden Classics?
Every month_____ If so, how many per month_____
Quarterly_____

* One calendar per household.

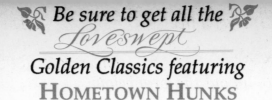

Be sure to get all the

Loveswept

Golden Classics featuring

HOMETOWN HUNKS

On sale in October

---

with him all over again. Not when she didn't have the strength to stop herself.

Jace bit back a sigh. "I think we'd better wait a couple of minutes."

"Why?"

"Because," he said, giving her a lopsided grin as he pressed her hips back against the DeSoto with his own. Her eyes went wide at the feel of him hard and straining against her softness. "If we go back now, everybody in Captain Jack's is going to know just how much I like you."

Six

Jace's therapy proceeded at a rate that pleased him but couldn't quite placate his urge to hurry back to baseball. Eighty miles away, the Chicago Kings were in second place in their division, playing adequate but uninspired ball. The Mishawaka Mavericks occupied their usual spot in the Class A standings—the cellar. It looked to Jace as though everybody needed a third baseman. He was allowed to do no more than take light batting practice.

Rebecca assured him that the injured knee was progressing very well. She stressed the importance of not trying to go back too soon.

Making progress with Rebecca outside the therapy room was slower going. In the nearly three weeks since their evening at Captain Jack's, she had allowed him to take steps to renew their friendship but had drawn the line after that. It was a line that blurred when he stole an occasional kiss or managed to remind her of the kind of passion they once had shared, but the boundary was there just the same.

All in all, Jace felt he really couldn't complain about the way things were going. He had known that starting over would be a slow process, but he felt he was making a solid foundation on which to build the rest of his life. It was sort of like hitting. A man didn't develop a perfect swing overnight.

It would all come together for him. He could feel it, feel that luck was gradually swinging to his side where Rebecca was concerned. Of course, the new Jace Cooper wasn't going to rely on luck to save the game for him.

Rebecca sat at her desk, going over the statistics for the proposed expansion of the physical therapy department, looking for places where she could cut corners without compromising patient care.

"Feel like breaking for coffee?" Dominique asked, sticking her head into the office.

Rebecca pulled her reading glasses off and dropped them onto the sea of paper that covered her desk. She made a face. "I feel like breaking something."

"I don't envy you your administrative duties," Dominique said, bumping the door open with her hip and carrying in a cafeteria tray with coffee and doughnuts on it.

"Nor should you."

Rebecca took in her friend's appearance at a glance. Dominique's mane of curly black hair was slicked back into a ponytail that blossomed behind her head like a bursting cattail. Beneath her standard white hospital jacket she wore a shimmering gold blouse and a black leather skirt that displayed her mile-long legs to perfection. Rebecca shook her head in amazement. "How do you do it, Dominique? I feel like a lab rat running around in this coat, and you look as though you belong on the cover of *Cosmopolitan*."

"It's called flamboyance," Dominique answered, sitting down and pouring a drop of cream into her coffee. "Your understated elegance is hidden by the coat. My flamboyance turns it into an accessory. Any other profound questions you want me to answer? About your love life, for instance?"

"I don't have a love life," Rebecca said on a groan. "I'm living in a state of limbo."

"Why is that?"

She sighed as she leaned back in her chair. "Jace tells me he's changed. He needs me to believe in him. I can see the changes, but I still can't bring myself to trust him. I'm scared."

"Understandable." Dominique nodded as she broke a sugared doughnut in two and nibbled on a piece. "For what it's worth, I've had my eye on Jace the Ace. He comes across like the genuine article to me, and I can spot a phony man before anyone else so much as catches a whiff of his aftershave."

Rebecca's mouth dropped into its natural sultry pout. "The trouble is, Jace never was a phony. He always meant what he said when he said it."

"But—?"

"But . . ." Rebecca's gaze was suddenly drawn through the window to the therapy room, where some kind of commotion had staff and patients gathering. "What in the world is going on out there?"

Dominique shrugged and dismissed it. "Let Max handle it. We're off duty."

Laughter sounded outside the office, and the crowd parted. Rebecca stared in astonishment as a robot motored toward her window. It was about four feet tall and nearly that wide, with a shiny aluminum canister for a body and a clear glass head like a giant light bulb. It wore an oversize white hospital jacket with the nametag "Dr. Merlin" pinned above the breast pocket.

A stethoscope hung around its neck. As it stopped outside the window, it blinked its lights at Rebecca and raised a hook-ended accordian arm in greeting.

"Where did *that* come from?" Dominique asked, amazed.

Rebecca shook her head, laughing. "I have reason to believe it came from my basement. Dad and Jace have been down there for weeks working on it."

They abandoned their coffee and went out into the exercise room to get a closer look. The robot wheeled around and approached Rebecca, the panel of buttons on its chest lighting up like a Christmas tree. It stopped a foot away from her, chattering and beeping, until a green-striped printout emerged from a slot in its midsection.

Hesitantly Rebecca reached out, tore the sheet of paper away, and read it aloud. "Patient: Rebecca Bradshaw. Dr. Merlin's diagnosis: Works too hard. Dr. Merlin prescribes: A night on the town with Jace Cooper."

Good-natured laughter rippled through the crowd that had assembled.

"That's sound medical advice, Rebecca," Dr. Cornish said, a grin splitting his plump, pleasant features.

"She doesn't date patients!" Bob Wilkes called emphatically from the whirlpool.

Mr. Peppy, the sweat sock hand puppet, suddenly popped into Rebecca's face, eyebrows waggling. "Doctor's orders, Ms. Bradshaw. A hot date with Jace the Ace. What do you say?"

"I say I don't discuss my private life with hosiery," she said dryly.

The robot came to life again, startling Rebecca so she jumped back. It blinked and bleeped and spat out another piece of paper. She pulled it away from the little machine, this time reading the printout to herself.

A smile curved up the corners of her mouth. Dr. Merlin promised a romantic dinner in a local establishment that boasted turn-of-the-century decor, Tiffany lamps, and superb aged steak, followed by a moonlight cruise down the St. Joseph River aboard the double-decker paddleboat *The Princess of Mishawaka.*

Who but Jace would be crazy enough to romance her with a robot? Who but Jace would be sweet enough? Who but Jace would know of her love for moonlight on the river?

"What's the verdict?" Mrs. Krumhansle asked from her position on the mat table.

Rebecca grinned. "I think I'll go out with Dr. Merlin."

"I don't think that would be a very good idea," Jace said, walking into the exercise room with a remote control box in his hands. "You know how you are with machines, Becca. Poor Merlin would be reduced to a bucket of bolts before the evening was over."

Rebecca laughed and shook a finger at him. "You're outrageous."

"I aim to please," he said, glowing with happiness. He had the distinct feeling that Rebecca was getting ready to erase that line she'd drawn between them.

"Well, aim your fanny at that exam table, Cooper," she ordered, taming her wide smile. "We have work to do around here."

The crowd began to break up, though a number of patients and staff seemed unusually reluctant to leave. Rebecca ignored them. Her relationship with Jace was the main topic of debate on the third floor of the hospital, overtaking even the gossip about the ward secretary and the handsome resident in orthopedics. She had decided the best way to handle the problem was to act as if it weren't a problem. She treated Jace's flirting as she treated any other patient's—outwardly at least.

Using the remote control, Jace parked his robot out of harm's way.

"You and Dad have done quite a job on that little monster," Rebecca said.

"Your dad is a genius. I just helped with the nuts-and-bolts stuff," Jace said, hoisting himself onto the table. "He's asked me to help him with the marketing after the baseball season is over."

"Really?" Was that a subtle way of telling her Hugh had faith in him sticking around, she wondered. "Lie flat on your back."

After removing his brace she lifted his left leg off the table, bent it at the knee, and rotated his foot with one hand while her other hand gently felt his injured joint, checking for meniscal damage.

"You never answered," he said.

"I never answered what?" Keeping his knee bent at about twenty degrees, she carefully pulled his leg forward, testing the integrity of the healing anterior cruciate ligament.

"Dinner and the cruise. Will you join me?"

"I don't date patients."

Chuckling, Jace shook his head. He craned his neck to catch a glimpse of her face. "That dog won't hunt, sweetheart. We've already been out together."

"That wasn't a date, that was a coincidence. As I recall, I told you I'd slug you if you called it a date."

The smile she gave him was secretive and teasing and so utterly feminine, it almost made Jace groan aloud. For once he was grateful when she took her hands off his body. Between her touch and the excitement of knowing she was on the brink of accepting him wholly, he was becoming damned aroused. It didn't help that he spent his nights reliving their lovemaking in his dreams. Memories of how warm and responsive she was in bed had sharpened his hunger for her to the point that he was ready to kidnap her if she didn't go out with him soon.

"Add two pounds for your progressive resistance exercises. You can start riding the bike for additional strengthening work, but be careful not to overdo it," Rebecca said as Jace sat up. To his ears only, she whispered, "We can talk about this date after work."

Jace fought back the urge to kiss her right there in front of her staff and patients. Instead he gave her a wink and slid off the table.

"I won't tell a soul," he whispered.

Rebecca watched him saunter toward the weight machine. Across the room several patients and staffers huddled together, arguing. Intending to break it up and send them back to work, Rebecca started toward them but brought herself up short as snatches of their conversation landed on her ears.

"That robot was a masterstroke."

"I say it's after the fact. You heard him say they'd already been out."

"And she said they hadn't, so all bets are still on."

"No way."

"Clear it with Jace."

"Clear what with Jace?"

All faces froze at the sound of Rebecca's voice. No doubt molten lava would have frozen at her tone. She stood with her hands planted on her hips, the look in her eyes preventing anyone from saying anything. Bob Wilkes sat in his wheelchair at the center of the group with a chart spread out on his lap. Rebecca stepped forward and snatched the paper up. PT POOL: IF AND WHEN WILL REBECCA GO OUT WITH JACE? was printed across the top in black marker.

The silence built around them. When Rebecca didn't move or speak but merely went on staring at the chart, some of the others murmured excuses and platitudes in voices as meek as church mice.

"It was just for fun."

"We didn't mean anything by it."

But all Rebecca could hear was one sentence she had picked up by accident. *Clear it with Jace.*

A fine rage built inside her until she thought she would burst at the seams. She turned on her heel and strode purposefully to the weight machine, where Jace was getting ready to strap his leg in. Throwing the chart in his face, she said, "In my office. Right now."

He followed her in and closed the door, watching silently as she yanked the cord on the venetian blinds, shutting out their would-be audience.

Rebecca turned and slapped at the chart in his hands. "You think this is a game? You think my life is a game? I should have known you would pull something like this!"

Jace threw the paper down on her desk, his expression stony. "I didn't have anything to do with this, Rebecca."

"You expect me to believe that?" she asked, incredulous. "You're the one who took bets on everything from boat races to babies being born. This has your name written all over it."

"I told you, I quit gambling."

She laughed, though she found no humor in the situation. She had been on the verge of forgiving and forgetting past indiscretions. "And I believed you, fool that I am."

Jace slammed his fist against the door, fury demanding a physical release. "Dammit, Becca, why can't you have a little faith in me? I've changed. I'm willing to prove it to you any way you want, but it would be nice if you'd just believe me for once. I admit I've made mistakes in my life. I'm sorry for them. Haven't you ever made a mistake?"

"Yes," she said bitterly, tears stinging her eyes. "I'm looking at him."

Jace stepped back as if she'd struck him. The air crackled with tension, hurt, and betrayal. In the next instant he was gone.

Rebecca slumped down on her chair, tears spilling through the barrier of her thick black lashes. She put her head down on her desk and sobbed, crying for her hurt, for the hurt look on Jace's face, for the cruel twist of fate that made her want to love a man she couldn't trust. Pain and confusion spilled out in the form of salty tears that stained her reports on the proposed expansion of the department. Losing all track of time, she cried as she hadn't cried in seven years.

When the tears were spent, Rebecca was so exhausted, she dozed for a few minutes. When she opened her eyes again, it was to see a sweat sock with a face peering at her over the edge of her desk. Turk Lacey, whom she knew was attached to the goofy thing that was staring at her, was nowhere within her range of vision, leading Rebecca to believe he was lying on the floor. What a strange, strange man he was.

Mr. Peppy made a sad face. "I made you cry. Sad am I, Rebecca, darling of my heart."

"I don't understand. What did you do, Mr. Peppy?" Rebecca asked hoarsely. Lord, I'm talking to a sweat sock, she thought.

"Jacer the Acer didn't make the pool. Turk Lacey was the fool behind that."

A sick feeling swirled in her stomach. "Jace didn't have anything to do with it?"

Mr. Peppy scrunched his painted face and shook his head, yarn hair bobbing.

"Oh, no," Rebecca whispered.

What little strength she had left seemed to seep out of her with a sigh. Tears welled in her eyes again. As much as she knew Jace needed her to believe in him, still she had turned around and accused him of something as juvenile as taking bets on their relationship. She had been so ready to believe the worst of him.

Holier than thou, aren't you, Rebecca?

It was a bitter voice from the past, one that accused her of sitting in judgment.

You're too hard on people, daughter.

Haven't you ever made a mistake?

Heaven help her, she'd made a million of them, Rebecca thought, squeezing her eyes shut against pain that was self-inflicted. She was no less judgmental of herself than she was of anyone else. If anything, the punishment she meted out to herself was even harsher. Forgiveness had never come easily to her, least of all when the one who needed forgiving was herself.

"Spacy Lacey is awfully sorry," Mr. Peppy said with a suspicious huskiness in his funny little voice. "He didn't mean to make you cry. He doesn't want to make you worry. He'll set things straight by and by."

Rebecca shook her head. "No, Mr. Peppy. I'm the one who made the real mistake. I'll have to fix things with Jace myself. I just hope he'll forgive me."

The day conspired against Rebecca. Phone calls to Muriel and Hugh failed to shed any light on Jace's whereabouts. She was informed by the Mavericks' batting coach that Jace had been to the ballpark and left again.

By the end of the day she was exhausted, disheartened, and depressed. For good measure, she gave herself another forty lashes of mental punishment as she prepared to lock up her office and leave for home.

Electronic bleeping and rattling accompanied Merlin as the robot rolled into the exercise room. Rebecca went to her door and opened it, staring at the chattering little machine as it motored toward her, backed her into the edge of her desk, then stopped. Lights flashing, it spewed out computer paper. With her heart lodged in her throat, Rebecca tore off the message and read it.

PLEASE ACCOMPANY ME, MISS BRADSHAW.

Not sure whether it was a friendly invitation or a royal command, Rebecca gathered up her purse and followed the robot, locking her office door behind her. Merlin led her down the hall to the elevator. When they reached the main floor, it buzzed toward the automatic doors that led out to the parking lot.

Jace stood leaning back against her blue Honda, the late afternoon sun turning his hair golden. Rebecca's heart bumped against her ribs. He looked so handsome to her, more so now than he had seven years ago. She liked the rough edges time had given his looks. Standing by her car in worn jeans and a dark blue shirt, he looked tough and utterly masculine. He straightened as their gazes met, tension squaring his shoulders.

"Hi."

"Hi," Rebecca said, as nervous as a teenager just discovering boys. Her ability to read people's moods deserted her as she looked at Jace, and a sense of panic shivered through her. What if he wouldn't accept her apology? What if he was fed up with her attitude?

Why did it matter so much?

She nibbled at her lip and pushed the question to the back of her mind.

"I'm sorry. I was wrong," she said.

Jace felt a tug at his heart. Rebecca looked like Anne Boleyn ready to face the executioner. He'd been angry enough that morning to volunteer for the job, but his temper had cooled. Actually, he'd vented it at batting practice, all but knocking the covers off the balls that were thrown at him. By the time he'd left the ballpark, the only thing that had mattered to him was being in love with her and wanting to spend his life with her. The new Jace Cooper wasn't going to back down just because of a misunderstanding.

"I shouldn't have accused you, Jace," Rebecca said, her green eyes pleading for forgiveness she didn't think she deserved.

Jace gathered her close, wrapping his arms around her and holding her like the precious treasure she was. She was his salvation. Memories of her love had gotten him through hell and lured him to take the second chance fate had offered. How could he not forgive her anything when he owed her so much? Burying his nose in the ebony silk of her hair, he kissed her ear and whispered, "It's okay, baby. I love you."

Rebecca squeezed her eyes shut and hugged Jace for all she was worth. It suddenly became very clear why his forgiveness had been so important to her. It had nothing to do with her sense of honor or fairness and everything to do with an emotion she had been trying hard to avoid. But now, held hostage in Jace's arms, there was nowhere left to run. The words came out of their own volition, and Rebecca accepted them as being as inescapable as fate. "I love you too."

It was true, whether she wanted it to be or not. The resignation came through in her voice. Jace shook off the hurt that threatened to descend again. Rebecca loved him. All he had to do was convince her he was worthy of that love. In time she would trust him.

Merlin broke the mood, suddenly bleeping and spinning around in circles. Her heart pounding, Rebecca all but leaped in Jace's arms.

"It's okay," he said, chuckling. "Merlin's still got a few bugs to work out of his system."

He managed to shut down the robot and with Rebecca's help packed him into the trunk of her car.

"Your dad and Muriel took Justin and a couple of his

buddies out for burgers," Jace explained as he lifted a wicker picnic basket from the asphalt. "I was hoping to interest you in a picnic." He lifted his dark eyebrows as he lifted the lid on the basket to let mouthwatering aromas escape. "Muriel really knows how to fry a chicken, and I can spread a blanket on the grass with the best of them."

Jace gave directions as Rebecca drove. They ended up out in the country on a secluded back road and parked in the drive of an empty pasture. It was a place that brought back nearly as many memories for Rebecca as the man beside her did. The summer of their ill-fated romance, they had come here more than once to spend time together. Sometimes they had made love. Sometimes they had only sat and talked, Jace listening patiently as Rebecca had talked about her hopes, her dreams, her insecurities, her troublesome relationship with her sister.

Silently they walked out into the field, both of them instinctively walking toward a copse of trees that would shield them from view from the road. On the other side of the trees a wide bank sloped gently to a stream. In the distance the sun hung low above a hill. They spread a patchwork quilt out on the grass as cardinals and whippoorwills sang in the trees behind them.

"This place brings back a lot of memories," Rebecca said softly.

Jace came to stand behind her, wrapping his arms around her and leaning his chin on her shoulder. "Not all of them are bad, are they, Becca?"

Tears stung her eyes. "No," she whispered. "None of them are. Not from this place."

Nuzzling through her hair, Jace kissed the soft, sensitive skin on the side of her neck, then along her strong jawline. Finally he turned her in his arms and captured her sweet, vulnerable mouth with his own. He kissed her slowly, deeply, drinking in the taste of her, trying to erase all but the best of her memories. His tongue stroked lazily against hers, reclaiming territory that had once been his and was his again. Forever this time, he vowed.

Rebecca didn't fight the desire that surged within her. She had been trying too long and too hard to hold it in check. Now it swept through her like a fire, searing her nerve endings, heating the surface of her skin, burning all the spots that ached for a man's touch. It had been forever since a man had made her feel this way. It had been since the last time she'd made love with Jace.

When he ended the kiss, he looked into her eyes. His own eyes were dark with passion, the color of the sky at twilight. "It's your call, Becca," he said earnestly. "There's nothing I want more than to make love with you right here, right now, but I won't seduce you. It has to be your choice."

Choice, Rebecca wondered. What choice was there to make? It seemed if ever there had been one, her heart had made it seven years ago. She loved Jace Cooper. Whether he would be hers for a summer or a lifetime didn't really matter. She'd wasted enough time as it was, fighting her desire to be with him.

Without saying a word she reached up and began to unbutton his shirt. Her gaze followed her fingers as they freed the buttons, revealing the smooth skin of his chest. When she reached the waistband of his jeans, Jace caught her wrists and pulled her hands up to roam freely over the ridges and planes of muscle that flexed and trembled at the touch of her long elegant fingers.

Rebecca's lips followed the trail her hands blazed.

•

Like whispered memories, she brushed delicate kisses across his skin. The taste of him sparked an instant response in her body, and the flames of desire burned hotter, searing away control and reserve and logic. The only logic in this act belonged to nature, and nature dictated she love this man with her heart and with her body. It was a law as old and time-honored as life itself.

There was no shyness, no hesitation as Rebecca undid Jace's fly. Time had passed, but she still knew his body as well as she knew her own. She tugged down his jeans and designer briefs, letting her kisses follow their descent to the tops of his thighs. Thinking only of pleasing him, she caressed the essence of him with her hands and mouth, kissing, teasing, tasting.

Jace groaned at the intense combination of pleasure and memory. How many nights since the accident had he dreamed of this woman and the beauty of the physical harmony that had once been between them? To have those dreams become reality brought on a rush of emotion that tore away his control.

With his hands on her arms, he dragged Rebecca up his body for another kiss, this one faster and harder than the last. With trembling fingers, he rid her of her blouse and bra, freeing her full breasts to his touch. He bent her back, and she arched upward, offering a taut nipple to his hot, eager mouth.

Rebecca gasped as sensation poured over her and through her. Jace's mouth tugging at her breast sent shock waves zipping along her nerve endings to converge in the suddenly aching emptiness between her thighs, an emptiness Jace sought to soothe as his hands peeled down her slacks and panties.

He stroked her intimately, his blunt-tipped fingers gently parting the sweet, warm petals of her flesh. As he lowered her body to the quilt, Rebecca lifted her hips to his touch and whispered his name while he explored the depth of her readiness. Instinctively she moved to the rhythm he set, her eyes drifting shut as he planted kisses on her stomach, her hip, the flesh of her inner thigh. Her hands clutched first at the blanket, then at his smoky blond hair as he kissed her as deeply and intimately as she had him.

"Oh, Jace, please," Rebecca whispered as he slid up along her body to kiss the pulsebeat in the base of her throat. She twined her long legs around his, inviting him to fill her with his rigid maleness. "Please."

"Are we safe, honey?"

"Yes. Oh, Jace, please. I want you so much."

"Have you dreamed about it, sweetheart, as I have? I've dreamed about making love with you, about you wanting me again. I've dreamed about how hot and tight you used to be, of how responsive you were."

Jace's words served to arouse Rebecca as much as his touch had. She slid her hand between their bodies to find him eager for her guidance. Biting her lip, she strained against him as he tried to ease into her.

"Easy, sweetheart," Jace murmured tenderly. His breath came in short, hard gasps as he sank into her flesh, careful to let her adjust to him an inch at a time until he was fully embraced by the silken glove of her womanhood. He fought the completion that threatened as she tightened around him in ripples of sensation. "Just relax, honey."

Rebecca wrapped her arms around him and buried her face against his throat as she climaxed. Whatever her misgivings about Jace, this was right, this was perfect. When they came together this way, their union was far more than physical. Their connection was between body *and* soul. The sensation was one of predestiny and pleasure—wonderful, indescribable pleasure.

The aftershocks hadn't even begun to subside when Jace started building the sensation again. He moved against her and inside her with a grace that was beautiful and natural. Her response was equally beautiful and natural. Her hips lifted to meet his deep thrusts, her breasts arched into the heat of his mouth. Her hands stroked his back and the taught muscles of his buttocks, teasing him, urging him. Her sighs of delight became whimpers and moans as sexual tension tightened inside her, building toward another explosion.

Jace kissed her ear. "I love you, sweetheart. I love to please you, honey."

Rebecca felt herself teetering at the edge of blissful oblivion. Jace told her how close he was to the same precipice. She remembered times in the past when they had taken each other over that edge. Jace remembered too. Now it beckoned them again, lured them closer with each stroke, with each murmured word, with each caress. Then Jace soared over it, calling her name, and Rebecca followed right behind him.

For a long time afterward they were silent. Rebecca turned on her side to face the stream and the sunset. Jace snuggled behind her, pulling the edge of the quilt up over them as the air began to cool.

"Where do we go from here?" he asked softly, tucking Rebecca's black hair behind the delicate shell of her ear. "You know I love you, Becca. I'll never hurt you again."

She rolled over and pressed two fingers to his lips. "No promises, Jace, please."

No promises you can't keep.

The hurt in his twilight-blue eyes cut at her heart.

"You still don't believe in me."

"I believe you've changed in a lot of ways, Jace."

"But not in the way that matters most." Angry, he moved away from her and started tugging on his clothes. "You're holding your breath waiting for me to revert to type, aren't you?"

Sadness welled in Rebecca's heart as she sat up with one hand clutching the quilt to her chest. What she and Jace had just shared had been wonderful, like nothing else she'd ever experienced. But she knew it wouldn't last. Jace was a man out of his normal environment; he needed her now. When the effects of his accident became nothing more than unpleasant memories and the Kings called him back to Chicago, he would go. He would leave her, just as he had before. He would go back to a lifestyle that didn't allow for memories, and she would be left with nothing but memories.

With his jeans on and his shirt hanging open, Jace stood and turned to look down at her. "Will you go to Chicago with me tomorrow?"

"Tomorrow? Why?"

"I want to show you why I changed and why the changes are permanent. You won't take my word for it, so I'll give you proof." *And pray to God you don't hate what I used to be so much that you won't be able to stand the sight of me.*

Rebecca frowned at the bitterness in his voice but nodded. Maybe what he had to show her would make a difference. Maybe it would tell her about the pain he'd gone through that had aged his beautiful blue eyes so. Maybe it would somehow free her heart to love him as completely as he wanted her to, as completely as she longed to.

Seven

They drove to Chicago in almost total silence. It was a cloudy Saturday morning with the threat of rain hanging heavy in the air. Rebecca drove, knowing Jace didn't even like to ride in a car since his accident, let alone drive. She had gathered from comments he'd made that he no longer possessed a driver's license—a real turnabout for a man who had once filled a three-car garage with sleek Italian sports cars.

Jace stared at the dull gray road that stretched out before them and at the gray horizon beyond it. He sat on the passenger's side, his fingers toying nervously with his seat belt, looking as if he were going to meet a fate worse than death. Lord, he as dying for a cigarette or a drink, or both. The need was always stronger on the days he went to visit Casey. It was then that panic would claw at his insides and the coward in him would beg for a shield to protect him from what he'd done.

He had never, *would* never give in to that need.

It was even worse with Rebecca sitting beside him. Soon he would have no secrets from her. He wondered

112

if it wouldn't have been better to have kept this reality to himself. The closer they came to Chicago, the more he believed he would rather have gone on with her being hesitant to trust him. There was every chance she would walk away once she found out the whole truth about his past. He didn't think he could live through that.

From the corner of his eye he studied Rebecca. She wore a white cotton blouse with a pattern of flowers and leaves embroidered and cut out across the bodice, revealing patches of creamy flesh. Her lavender skirt was gauzy and gathered delicately at the waist. Her profile was worthy of any antique cameo he'd ever seen.

She was lovely, much more so than she realized. One of Becca's greatest insecurities had always been that she was all intellect and no femininity. Tenderness welled in Jace's heart. He had never known a woman who had more claim to the description of feminine. To him she was everything a woman should be. More than anything, he wanted to spend the rest of his life with her. He understood everything about her—her strengths, her fears, her flaws—and he loved her for all of them. If he lost her . . .

If he lost Rebecca and Justin, it would probably be no more than he deserved, he thought as he directed her off the expressway.

Rebecca could sense the tension building in Jace with every mile. Still she asked no questions about their destination. Obviously he did not want to talk about it. Even after she had parked the car in the lot of the beautiful modern hospital in a posh Chicago suburb, Jace offered no explanation. They crossed the parking lot together in silence as the rain began.

Inside, the hospital was Saturday-quiet. There was no bustle of people waiting for appointments or arguing over accounting errors on their bills. The weekend staff, made up of nurses and bleary-eyed residents, went about their business with calm efficiency. Visitors talking in hushed tones lingered in a lobby worthy of a luxury hotel.

Jace bypassed the information desk and went directly to a bank of elevators. Tapping the toe of his black loafer impatiently against the smooth marble floor, he rammed his fists into the pockets of his pleated gray trousers and waited for the elevators doors to open.

As they rode up to the tenth floor, Rebecca watched his pallor increase. The haunted look in his eyes made her want to go to him and put her arms around him. Whether that desire was to comfort or be comforted, she wasn't sure. Her own nerves were jangling. She'd never known Jace to be so solemn about anything. He hadn't even cracked a smile since they'd made love the night before.

It frightened her how alone she felt now that Jace had withdrawn into himself. What was going to become of her when he left?

The elevator doors opened on a special care unit. The nurses' station sat at the center with rooms situated around it like spokes around the hub of a wheel. Fluorescent light glowed above the wood-paneled, pentagon-shaped desk area. The nurse manning the station must have been fifty. She looked big enough and mean enough to play tackle for the Bears, but when she glanced up and saw Jace, her features melted into a motherly smile.

"Hi, stranger! We've missed you around here," she said in a clear, rough voice that she automatically toned down out of deference to the patients in the rooms around her.

"Hi, Sophie," Jace said, forcing the corners of his mouth up. "I can't get here as often as I'd like to. I'm living in Mishawaka now."

"So we heard." She made a face. "Management bone-heads. Smart money says you'll be back for the stretch drive. Lindenfelder's defense stinks up the place. He couldn't match you at third if he was twins."

"We'll see," he said, dismissing the topic as if it were as unimportant as the weather. "How's Casey?"

The light in Sophie's eyes immediately dimmed to a soft glow of sympathy. She couldn't quite muster a smile for him. It was a look Rebecca had seen many times. She had been on the receiving end of it again and again as disease had slowly robbed her mother of life. She herself had given that look to patients, to families of patients, when a prognosis couldn't meet their hopeful expectations. Her heart ached for Jace, even though she didn't know what his connection to this patient was.

"No change," the nurse said. "I'm sorry, Jace. He's holding his own. That gives us something to hope for."

With a shaky sigh, Jace nodded and turned away. His hand reached back for Rebecca's. She latched onto it as if it were a lifeline and followed him away from the desk to one of the rooms.

Who was Casey, she wondered. A family member or a friend? A man or a woman? Why had Jace never spoken of this person before? What kind of medical problem were they about to face? Questions flew through her mind with the speed of light, but there was no time to search for answers. She caught a glimpse of the room through the window that faced the nurses' station, but all she saw was the foot of the bed and a chair. They stepped inside and Jace closed the door behind them.

It was the room of a patient who had been there for some time, Rebecca thought as she glanced around. Get-well cards were pinned to a bulletin board on the sterile white wall. Children's crayon drawings of animals and spaceships and baseball players were taped beneath it. There was an autographed Chicago Kings pennant above the bed. A team picture stood on the small metal cabinet against the far wall beside a thriving African violet and a photograph of someone's parents. An afghan crocheted of blue and gold yarn was neatly folded at the foot of the bed.

"Becca," Jace said softly, "this is Casey Mercer."

He was a handsome man of perhaps twenty-two or twenty-three, with strong features, short dark hair cropped close to his head, and thick long eyelashes that curled boyishly along his cheek. Rebecca had a feeling his eyes would be brown, but she couldn't see them.

Casey Mercer was in a coma. Machines monitored his vital signs as he lay unmoving on the bed. He was thin. Skin that had the shiny translucence of fine porcelain was stretched over bones that were too prominent.

Jace went to him and took Casey's long, frail hand in his own. "Hey, Mercer," he said in a soft, teasing voice. "Red alert. There's a beautiful woman in the room. I brought my friend, Rebecca. Remember? I told you about her. I figured it was time I told her about you."

The young man remained motionless, but Jace went on speaking as though it weren't a one-sided conversation.

"I should have warned you, huh? You could have dressed up. Hell, you're too pretty as it is. An old guy like me hardly stands a chance. Besides, you don't need to steal my girl when you've got a bevy of beautiful nurses waiting on you hand and foot, right? One of these days I'm going to come up here and catch you chasing them around the bed."

Rebecca blinked back tears as she watched Jace pause to swallow the lump in his throat. She didn't know Casey Mercer, didn't know what Jace's connection to the young man was, but she didn't need to. She could feel everything Jace was feeling—helplessness, anger, sorrow. His pain was her pain, because she loved him.

"The team needs you, kid," Jace said thickly. "You'd better get your butt in gear and snap out of it. You know how you're always telling me you'll be the best damn shortstop ever to wear a jockstrap. Well, you've got to back up bull like that, Mercer, otherwise people will think you're just as full of it as I am."

Silence was the only retort Jace received.

Gently he placed Casey's limp hand back on the bed. He tapped his friend's cheek affectionately with his fingertips.

"Hang in there, buddy," he whispered, rubbing a knuckle at the moisture under his eyes. "I'm so sorry I screwed up your life."

They were the only people in the tenth-floor lounge. No one had even bothered to turn the lights on. The room was gloomy with shadows. Rain washed down the plate glass windows in silvery sheets. Jace sat on a chrome-legged table near a window, staring out at nothing, trying to gather his thoughts. He braced one foot on the seat of an orange plastic chair. Rebecca sat watching him, patiently waiting for him to speak. Thunder rumbled in the distance.

"It's hard, you know," Jace said softly, still focusing his gaze outside. "He's just a kid. Nothing but guts and instinct. I never saw anything like him on the infield. Quick as a cat."

"What happened?" Rebecca asked, speaking in the whisper hospital lounges seemed to inspire.

A muscle tugged in Jace's cheek as the pain cut through him. "Me. I was his idol. Some idol," he said bitterly, his mouth twisting in a grimace of disgust. "Because of me, he may spend the rest of his life in that room."

"The accident," Rebecca deduced aloud. "He was with you?"

Jace didn't answer her right away. He looked down and traced a finger around the edge of a cheap glass ashtray, desperately wishing he had a cigarette. When he spoke again, he started the story at the beginning.

"When I got called up to the show, I figured I had the world by the tail. I was hot, popular. Everybody wanted to know Super Cooper. I was making more money in a year than some small countries. It's not an excuse, but you have to understand what money like that can do, how it can make you feel invincible. I threw it around like candy at a parade. You know, I always did like to play fast and loose with my cash. Easy come, easy go." He flashed a grin that died quickly. "I liked to have a good time. I liked everybody to have a good time.

"Most of it's gone now. What I didn't gamble away or throw away on bad business deals went to Casey. This is an excellent hospital for the kind of care he needs. His folks couldn't begin to afford it, and his insurance wouldn't cover it all.

"Casey came up last season from the triple-A team in Lexington. It was like *déjà vu* for me. Everybody wanted to know Casey. Right off the bat he started hanging around with me. No party was complete without Jace the Ace and Casey.

"The night of the accident we'd been out ramming around in my Porsche, party hopping. He asked me if he could drive because he'd just ordered one of his own, and he wanted to practice impressing women. I let him, even though I knew he wasn't in any shape to get behind the wheel. 'Course, I wasn't any better off. We were doing eighty-five on the Dan Ryan Expressway, and Casey looked over at me with this big bright grin on his face and said, 'Don't you know, Jace, I want to be just like you. You're my hero.'"

He could still see Casey's handsome young face glowing with life in the lights from the instrument panel. The image of that smile was frozen for all time in his mind, just as those words would forever ring in his ears.

"That was the last thing he ever said to anybody."

Rebecca closed her eyes against the pain she felt for Jace and for Casey Mercer. She remembered Jace at Casey's age, brash, charming Jace who had thought his luck would never run out. Now he sat staring out the hospital window struggling under the weight of responsibility, not only for his own mistakes but for Casey Mercer's as well.

"There's nothing quite like nearly killing someone to make you take a good hard look at yourself," he said sardonically. "I came out of the crash with a bum knee and some broken ribs and a second chance I didn't deserve. I'm not going to screw it up. Something good has to come out of this, or what happened to Casey will all have been for nothing. I can't let that happen."

Rebecca couldn't find it in her to condemn him; Jace had certainly done a good enough job of condemning himself. For once she didn't try to sit in judgment. Jace had been through hell. He would go on paying for this mistake for the rest of his life. He didn't need her to tell him he shouldn't have let Casey Mercer get behind the wheel. In fact, she found she wanted to blame someone else. Why had the host of the party they'd been to let either one of them drive?

She was well aware of the fact that at some other point in time she would have jumped on her soapbox and harangued Jace. He was a star. He was in the public eye. He should have set a better example for the kids who looked up to him. But she had watched him struggle. She had seen him hurt. He was just a man, as vulnerable to making mistakes as any other man.

Being a star didn't make him immune or immortal. He was facing that truth now, and Rebecca's heart ached with love for him.

Jace didn't need her censure now. He needed her support and her love.

She reached out and took his hand, squeezing it as she gave him a game smile. "You can make it count, Jace," she said softly.

Her strength pulled Jace's out from under him. His face tightened as he turned more toward the window. He sniffed and swallowed hard. Strain shredded the soft fabric of his voice. "I never meant to hurt anybody. Not Casey, not you."

"I know," Rebecca whispered, coming out of her chair to put her arms around him. "I know."

"Looks as though Muriel and Dad are out on the town," Rebecca said as she glanced at the note Muriel had left on the heavy oak library table. A fat black-and-white cat pounced on the table, snatched the note from her hand, and dashed off with it. "It still surprises me, but I'm glad they've started seeing each other." It was Jace's doing, she reminded herself.

"Do you think they're getting serious?" Jace asked as he glanced through his mail.

"I don't know." Like any child, small or grown, it was difficult for Rebecca to imagine her father in a romantic situation. "They have fun together."

Jace gave her a sharp look as a thought suddenly occurred to him. "Who's watching Justin?"

"He's spending the weekend with a friend," she said, trying not to feel too pleased with Jace's concern.

Despite what she'd seen that afternoon, she still didn't want to become too used to having Jace around. The fact remained that he wanted to return to Chicago. If his knee held up, he would be leaving, and changed or not, there was no guarantee he would come back.

"I've been working on a present for him," Jace said, his expression softening into a genuine smile for the first time in nearly twenty-four hours.

Stepping over a pair of kittens wrestling in the middle of the hall, he led Rebecca back toward his rooms. She took pleasant note of the fact that the house no longer smelled musty and feline. The scent of potpourri hung in the air instead.

"It's kind of a present for you too," Jace said. "Wait here."

Rebecca stopped where he instructed her, just outside the door to his sitting room. Seconds later she was confronted by a mechanical dog.

It was about the size of a beagle and ran on treads, the way Merlin the robot did. Its ears looked like miniature satellite dishes, its tail was an antenna. The thing may not have had fur or fleas, but it certainly did resemble a dog. Jace had carefully painted on big brown eyes and a happy mouth. He had even hung a collar around its neck. It stopped at Rebecca's feet, bobbed its head, and barked at her from a little speaker set in its chest.

"Oh, Jace, it's wonderful!" she exclaimed. She dropped down on her knees to get a closer look, but was careful not to touch it or make it go haywire. It extended a pink rubber tongue and licked her hand.

"Your father did the electrical and computer work," Jace explained. "I designed the body and did the mechanics. It won't make a mess on the rug or bite—not even someone who isn't mechanical."

Leaning against the doorjamb, automatically taking his weight off his healing knee, Jace worked the buttons and switches on the remote control panel. He put the little metal mongrel through its paces in the hall—

running it backward and forward, making it bark and wag its tail. He showed her how it could retrieve a metal bone using the magnet in its nose.

Outraged, Muriel's cats scattered in every direction, fleeing wild-eyed from the monster.

"I know it's not as good as a real dog, but I thought it would do for a while," Jace said. He directed the dog back into his room and turned it off, setting the remote control on an end table.

He was tempted to say his creation would do until he, Rebecca, and Justin officially became a family and moved into a house with a yard big enough to keep a dog outside. That was his dream, one he wanted very badly to realize—to be a father to Justin and a husband to Rebecca. But he held back from telling her.

After leaving the hospital neither one of them had said much. He had been deeply touched and given hope by her initial reaction to his story, but he kept telling himself that didn't mean he was home free.

Rebecca went to kiss his cheek. She could hardly speak for the knot in her throat. How sweet of Jace to try to make a little boy's dream come true. With everything else that was preying on his mind these days, she certainly wouldn't have expected this. "Justin will love it. Thank you."

Jace slipped his arms around her. "He's a terrific kid. I'm crazy about him."

"He thinks the world of you," she said softly, focusing her gaze on a button on his dark blue shirt. She didn't say it worried her that Justin had become so attached to him. What was the point? It would only hurt Jace's feelings, and she would still have to deal with Justin's disappointment when Jace went back to the big league.

"Becca," Jace whispered, everything inside him going still with anticipation, "is Justin my son?"

Rebecca could feel the tension in him as he waited for her answer; it trembled in the muscles of his arms and vibrated subtly in the air around him. It seemed it was the day for revealing secrets. Jace had opened the door on his. He was asking her to do the same. She couldn't deny him.

Actually, she found she wanted to tell him the truth, even though it hurt her to bring up that part of the past. She needed to share it with Jace. He was, as he had been so long ago, her friend . . . and more. Instinctively she knew he would understand in a way no one else ever had.

"Becca?"

"No," she whispered, looking up into his indigo eyes with an expression that was akin to regret. "He's not your son, Jace. He's not mine either."

Jace stared at her, confused. "What? What do you mean he's not your son? You're his mother."

Rebecca moved out of his embrace to pace restlessly around the small room with its sinister-looking Victorian furniture. "No, I'm not—not biologically. My sister, Ellen, is his mother." She laughed without a trace of humor. "That is to say, she gave birth to him."

"Ellen?" That explained Justin's resemblance to Becca. One of the few things Jace remembered about Rebecca's younger sister was that she was nearly a carbon copy of Becca. And the boy's blue eyes? Well, they were nothing more than a coincidence. Plenty of people had blue eyes. Hugh Bradshaw had blue eyes.

Jace suddenly felt a bit foolish for having been so sure he was Justin's father. Foolish and sad. He felt as if he'd lost something that had never really been his. He tried to set his feelings aside as questions filled his head.

"Then where is she?" he asked. "Why does Justin call you Mom?"

Rebecca ran a hand through her hair and sighed tiredly. "Justin doesn't know. I think a little boy would find it hard to understand why his mother would simply leave and never come back."

It was impossible for her to say it and not sound bitter toward her sister. At the same time she was filled with such guilt, every inch of her body ached with it. The conflicting emotions brought tears up to sting her eyes.

Jace halted her pacing, gently taking hold of her shoulders and turning her to face him once more. "What happened?" he asked softly, then waited patiently for her to compose herself and her agitated thoughts.

"It was a few weeks after you left for Chicago," she finally began. "Ellen was supposed to be getting ready to go back to college, something she wasn't very enthusiastic about, but Dad insisted his daughters have a college education. Ellen wasn't much of a student. It didn't help matters that I had gone before her and graduated early.

"She came to see me at the hospital and told me she wasn't going back to school because she was pregnant. We had a horrible fight about responsibility and letting Dad down. She said she didn't care. She was sick of living in my shadow and never measuring up. In the end she left."

"Where did she go?"

"We never knew. We didn't hear from her for months, didn't have any idea where she was, if she was alive or—When she came back, Justin couldn't have been more than three or four days old. She handed him to me and said I would undoubtedly be a perfect mother since I was perfect at everything else." She could still hear the resentment in her sister's tone of voice. It still hurt. "We arranged for me to legally adopt Justin, then she left. We haven't seen her since."

"She's never come back to see Justin?" Jace asked, incredulous at the thought that a mother could care so little about her child, especially a child he had become so attached to.

"Not once. She's never so much as sent him a birthday card. She made it clear she wants nothing to do with him."

"What about his father?"

Rebecca shook her head sadly. "We don't know who he is. Ellen refused to tell anyone."

She walked away from Jace and went to stand by the window, where crisp new curtains framed the view of a dark, rainy evening. Even though it wasn't cold, she wrapped her arms around herself to ward off a chill.

"Legally, Justin is and always will be mine. Still, I shouldn't have misled you, Jace. I like to pretend none of that trouble with Ellen ever happened, that Justin is my son and I'm his real mother. But someday I'm going to have to tell him." Despair swelled inside her and choked her words in her throat as she said, "Then I won't be able to pretend anymore."

The tears that spilled from her eyes soaked into Jace's dark blue shirt when he turned Rebecca and folded his arms around her. They soaked into his soul as well. He hurt for her, with her, because he loved her. He knew her pain and her uncertainties. All he wanted was to comfort and protect her.

"You're his mother, Becca, in every way that counts."

"Sometimes I wonder what would have happened if I had offered Ellen support that day she came to my office, instead of getting on my high horse. I drove my own sister away because I had to be judge and jury. Then there's a selfish part of me that's glad about what happened because it gave me Justin. I love him so much."

She lifted her head, her emerald eyes glittering with

tears and pain. Her soft, sweet mouth trembled with emotion. "Yesterday you asked me if I'd ever made a mistake. Jace, I've made so many . . ."

And she'd punished herself for every one of them. Over and over. Rebecca had never been as hard on anyone as she was on herself. Jace knew that. Her sense of perfection was tied in with her sense of duty and her sense of responsibility. Because she didn't want to let anyone down, she didn't allow herself to make mistakes.

Smiling tenderly, he brushed her tears away with his thumbs as he framed her face with his hands. "Making mistakes only proves you're human, sweetheart. I couldn't love you if you weren't human. And I *do* love you, Becca."

Jace lowered his head the two inches necessary to press his lips to hers. She tasted of tears and vulnerability. He drank in the taste and offered what strength he had left after a long and trying day. He offered comfort and consolation, empathy and understanding.

No one knew more about making mistakes than Jace did. One of the biggest he'd ever made was leaving Rebecca behind all those years ago. Now he kissed her in an effort to make the past go away, to take them to a place where nothing else mattered but their love.

Rebecca took what he offered gladly, greedily. Tonight it didn't matter that the future was uncertain or the past full of hurt. She opened herself to Jace and the kind of magic only he could give her, holding nothing back in their kiss. She gave him everything she was, everything she had been.

"Stay with me tonight, Becca," he murmured, holding her close and kissing the black hair that curtained her ear like a raven's wing. "I need you. I need to hold you."

Her heart beat with a sense of relief. The thought of going home to spend the night in a lonely bed made her shiver. There had been so many nights like that. She needed to be with Jace. Some higher power had made them soul mates. That had never been more clear to her than now, when they had both bared their most painful secrets.

"Say you'll stay all night, Becca," Jace whispered, his hands sliding over her supple back.

A smile curved Rebecca's mouth upward ever so slightly as she looked at him. "I wouldn't want you to get into trouble with Muriel."

He smiled back and rubbed the tip of his aquiline nose against hers. "She doesn't do a bed check."

"Good," she said, sobering. She ran a cool hand along the plane of his cheek, noting the lines of strain and experience that added character to his handsomeness. "Because I don't plan on going anywhere until dawn."

Moving into Jace's bedroom, they shut the door in the faces of two curious tabbies that had wandered into the sitting room. In the back of her mind Rebecca registered the fact that the walls had been given a fresh coat of beige paint and the heavy green drapes had been replaced. But her attention was focused on Jace.

They had come together before out of desire. Their need now was different but no less intense. This need was one to comfort and be comforted, to give strength and take it.

They undressed each other slowly, kissing and caressing as they went. Jace sat on the bed as he undid the buttons that ran down the back of Rebecca's white cotton blouse. His lips trailed down the valley of her spine, lingering just above the waistband of her skirt. He nibbled at the downy-soft flesh as his fingers dealt with a button and a zipper. Her breath fluttered in her throat at the feel of the gauzy skirt sliding down over her hips and thighs. Dizziness swirled in her head when his lips followed the descent of her white silk tap pants over the graceful line of her hip.

Jace stood behind her then, his hands stroking the smooth bare flesh of her stomach and lower. She sighed and pressed her head back against his shoulder as his fingers combed through the thatch of ebony curls that hid her most feminine secrets. His arousal pressed into her back. She moved against him, wanting him, needing to be one with him.

When they stretched out across the mattress of the big mahogany bed, there was no sense of urgency, only the desire to be close. One long kiss faded into another and another, and the only sound was that of the rain that came steadily down outside the windows. Night closed around the old house like a black satin cloak, leaving the lovers in the soft, colorful glow of a single old Tiffany lamp.

Rebecca felt the past and all its hurts recede as Jace's hands and mouth soothed and aroused her at once. He knew every inch of her body, every place to touch and tease. He sought them all out and gave each his full attention, then allowed Rebecca to do the same with his body. Time stretched on and on. Neither noticed or cared.

When Jace finally mounted her, he let Becca take his full length in one smooth, slow stroke. They were still for a long moment as they savored their union and the sense of completion that came with it, a completion that was uniquely theirs.

Finally nature intervened. Rebecca's body tugged at Jace's, silently begging for release. He groaned and rocked his hips against hers. She sighed and arched up against him.

Their loving was slow and gentle, each movement

designed to prolong the pleasure as well as heighten it. Rebecca felt like a finely tuned instrument being played by a master musician. It was a sweet, tender melody, one that touched the most vulnerable corner of her heart, one that built slowly toward what she knew would be a soaring crescendo.

She straddled Jace, moving on him as he leaned back against the headboard of the bed. Her fingers dug into his muscular shoulders as she took him into her, deeper and harder with each stroke. Jace clutched her to him as their pleasure crested powerfully and left them floating on a wave of weakness and bliss.

Sated and relaxed for the first time in hours, they lay together, sharing a pillow. They listened to the rain and the mournful sound of a cat meowing at the back door.

"Can I make a confession?" Jace asked softly. He reached up a hand to comb back a lock of her hair.

"Haven't we done enough of that for one night?" Rebecca didn't want anything to intrude on this time, not the past, not the future.

Jace's smile was sheepish as he ignored her question. "I was disappointed when you told me Justin isn't mine. I want us to have children together, Becca. I want the love we make to create something even more beautiful than it has."

A sharp sense of longing ran through Rebecca. She wanted that too. She couldn't count the times she had wished she had given birth to Justin, and, although she had never admitted it, Jace was the only man she could have pictured as the father of her child. Sometimes it was hard for her to look at Justin and not imagine him as Jace's and her son.

Those were feelings she tried hard to ignore. She couldn't afford dreams like that one. They meant investing heavily in a future that was uncertain. Jace wanted to build on the foundation of the changes he had struggled to make within himself. That was an admirable desire. But Rebecca could too easily remember the past promises that lay broken with the pieces of a young girl's heart. And, too, there was a part of her that didn't want to be a part of Jace's penance. If her relationship with him was tied to his sense of guilt about Casey Mercer and his own past, what would happen when the ache of that guilt dulled?

Jace didn't comment on her lack of response. He warded off the hurt by simply ignoring Rebecca's silence and telling himself they would be a family, a growing, loving family. All they needed was time. He couldn't heal the wounds overnight, nor could he expect Becca to forget them.

Leaning on his elbows, Jace gazed down at her, his eyes midnight blue. "I love you, Becca. I've never said that to another woman."

"I love you," Rebecca whispered, reaching up to touch the silvery strands of his hair that spilled across his forehead. She had never said those words to another man; something told her she never would. For better or worse, Jace Cooper was the man who had captured her heart. She could only hope this time he wouldn't break it.

He leaned down and brushed the softest of kisses across her mouth. "You're everything a man could ever want. I don't deserve you, but I'll be damned if I'll let you go again."

Then he switched off the Tiffany lamp, took Rebecca in his arms, and proved his love to her in the only way he could.

Eight

"Feelings" blasting from an electric organ—complete with boom-chukka rhythm sounds—was not what Rebecca was used to hearing first thing in the morning. Her head came up off the pillow. Beside her, Jace slept on, magnificently naked, having kicked the sheets off. His ashblond head was burrowed under his pillow. Rebecca's thoughts scattered as she feasted on the sight.

He was all lines and angles and lean muscle—except for a gorgeously rounded backside. He grumbled in his sleep and turned from his belly onto his side so he was facing her. Rebecca's heart lodged at the base of her throat. She saw bodies every day—male, female, in shape, out of shape—but she had yet to come across a shape that made her mouth go dry the way Jace Cooper's did. The scars he had acquired over the past seven years only enhanced his masculinity.

Jace was an athlete in every sense of the word. He was beautifully made and possessed strength and stamina. Oh, boy, did he have stamina, Rebecca thought, her cheeks blooming with the memories. When Jace made love to her, it was magical. Nothing and no one could compare. When they made love, it was as if the past had no power over them, as if nothing mattered but the beautiful harmony between them.

Lying on her side, studying Jace in the early morning light, Rebecca wished she could feel secure knowing he was that one special person.

Suddenly her face dropped. She had spent the entire night in Jace's arms, and now it was morning and she was trapped in Jace Cooper's room with his landlady sitting out in the hallway playing "As Time Goes By" on the organ. His landlady, who had strictly forbidden him to have any hanky-panky go on in the room he rented from her.

"Jace, Jace, wake up!" Rebecca whispered urgently, poking him in the belly.

"Mmmm . . . again, sweetheart?" he mumbled in a low, lazy voice, rolling on his back. "Let me sleep just five more minutes."

Rebecca straddled him and pulled the pillow off his face. "Will you wake up?"

Jace's eyelids rose as lazily as his smile. Rebecca leaned over him, her black hair mussed wildly around her head. Naturally, his gaze was drawn downward to her full breasts with their large, dark rose-colored nipples. It wasn't at all difficult to remember how they had tasted, how they had felt in his mouth. He was also very aware of the heat of her femininity pressing softly against his bare belly. Lord, to share a bed with this woman for the rest of his life would be like heaven on earth.

In a smoky morning voice he said, "For a view like this I'll not only wake up, I'll jump through flaming hoops if you want me to."

"This is hardly the time for you to get turned on." Rebecca scowled at him and started to move away, but

Jace clamped his hands to her waist and held her where she was, his thumbs rubbing seductively against the soft skin of her tummy.

"I always thought morning was the perfect time," he said. "Especially when I wake up to find a beautiful naked woman sitting on my—"

"Jace Cooper," she whispered, her face flaming, "your landlady is practically right outside the door."

Jace shook his head, fighting back a devilish grin. "I'm not into threesomes. Becca, you surprise me."

She grabbed her pillow and thumped him in the face with it. "I'll surprise you all right—"

The next thing Rebecca knew, she was flat on her back and Jace's body was lovingly pressing hers down into the mattress. It happened so fast, she didn't even have time to squeal in surprise. She stared up at him as Muriel segued into "You Light Up My Life."

"Jace, this is serious," she said, trying to keep his mind on the topic. "What are we going to do?"

He bent his head and whispered a scenario in her ear that made her go weak.

"I meant about Muriel," she said, trying her best to ignore the way Jace was nipping at her collarbone. "If she catches me sneaking out of your room, she'll be furious with you."

"Then I guess I'll just have to keep you prisoner here in my bedroom. Mmmm, I like that idea," he said against her breast. He raised his head, his hair falling into blue eyes that gleamed with mischief. "Will you let me tie you up?"

"Jace!"

He slid up her body, growling and chuckling devilishly. As his arousal probed the juncture of her thighs, he stuck his tongue in her ear.

"This isn't funny."

"I agree," he said on a groan. "Wrap your legs around my hips, sweetheart."

A heat wave swept over her body at his words, but Rebecca refused to comply. "Muriel is from a different generation. She will not find it the least amusing that I spent the night with you. She'll probably throw you out."

Jace nibbled at the corner of her frown. "Then I'll have to come live in your bedroom. I'll let you tie me up."

"You ought to be *locked* up," she said, giggling as he tickled her ribs.

"Come on, honey," Jace cajoled in his most persuasive tone. He slid his hand between their bodies and made her gasp as his fingers found her most sensitive flesh. "Open up for me, baby. I can't think of a more wonderful way to start the morning than making love with you. And we can be as loud as we want. No one on earth could hear us above Muriel's playing."

The music stopped abruptly. Rebecca took advantage of Jace's surprise to scramble out from under him and off the bed. As she scavenged for her clothes, the organ burst into "Some Enchanted Evening."

"She's improved since she got her hearing aid, don't you think?" Jace asked, sitting back against the headboard and admiring the view as Rebecca bent over to pick up her panties.

"You'll have to go out in the hallway and distract her so I can sneak out the back door," Rebecca said as she struggled with the buttons that ran down the back of her blouse. This hardly seemed like the time to critique Muriel's organ playing.

"Whatever you say, sweetheart." Jace stepped off the bed and sauntered toward the bedroom door as naked as the day he was born.

Wild-eyed, Rebecca jumped in front of him, plastering her back against the door. "For heaven's sake, put some clothes on! I said to distract her, not give her a coronary!"

"You're the expert," he said, his warm gaze traveling the length of her, taking in her long legs and white silk tap pants. He planted a hand on either side of her head and leaned toward her until their lips practically brushed when he spoke. "You sure know how to distract me."

Rebecca closed her eyes against the involuntary surge of desire his nearness evoked, and groaned in frustration. It was all she could do to keep from running her fingers through his chest hair. Sometimes she thought her weakness for him was more dangerous than any chemical addiction. It was certainly as strong. "Jace . . ."

"Okay," he said, running a forefinger along the sleek line of her jaw. "I'll get dressed. I'll behave myself. You have to give me a good-morning kiss first."

The look she leveled at him was patently unamused.

"Just a little one," he said with a sweet smile. He brushed her hair back behind her ear. "You don't want to make me feel like a cheap one-night stand, do you?"

"Heaven forbid." Rebecca's tone was dry, but her eyes twinkled.

Wrapping her arms around his neck, she tilted her head up and kissed him, fully expecting him to try again to lure her back to bed. When he didn't, when he kept the kiss tender, she was surprised. She searched his face and was stricken yet again by the age in those indigo eyes she knew so well.

"I don't think I thanked you for staying with me yesterday," he said softly. "I don't just mean last night. I mean—"

"I know what you mean."

"I wasn't sure how you would feel about me after meeting Casey."

"I love you," she said, amazed by how simple those

words sounded. There was nothing simple at all about her relationship with Jace or the feelings that tangled inside her, leaving her feeling uncertain.

"Past mistakes and all?" he asked.

"We can't change the past," she said sadly. How much easier their lives would have been had they been able to go back in time. She could have been spared a broken heart. Jace could have been spared a broken life.

Rebecca couldn't change the past, nor was she willing to forget it, Jace thought. She might have been in love with him, but she still had reservations about him. He could see it in her eyes. He could hear the subtle edge in her voice that asked him not to probe too deeply or push too hard.

"Maybe we should talk about the future, then," he said, knowing he was crossing a line, knowing she would back away from the issue. Funny, he thought, he'd never considered himself a masochist.

Rebecca gave him a look designed to be teasing, but she wouldn't quite meet his eyes. "I think we're a little underdressed to have a serious discussion."

Jace glanced down. She had a point. It was difficult to have an important talk standing naked while one's landlady played a tango on the organ in the hall. Maybe this wasn't the right time for their talk. He could content himself to going on with Rebecca as they were for a while, giving her time to come to trust him, giving her time to see the love he was offering now wasn't a shallow imitation but the genuine article—straight from his heart.

"I suppose you're right," he said, stepping back. He picked her skirt up off a chair and handed it to her. "Here. You'll be less conspicuous sneaking out if people can't see your underwear."

She pulled his briefs off the doorknob and tossed

them to him with a wry smile. "And you'll be less conspicuous if people can't see your . . . attributes."

They dressed quickly, hoping Muriel would quit practicing and go to the kitchen for her daily dose of oatmeal and stewed prunes. To their dismay, she played on and on with exceptional enthusiasm, going through her entire repertoire. Jace and Rebecca sat on the fainting couch in his sitting room playing "Name That Tune" as they waited.

Finally the last few bars of "A Groovy Kind of Love" faded away. Jace went to the door and stuck his head out, then drew it back in.

"The coast is clear."

"I'd better make a break for it," Rebecca said, clutching her sandals in her hand.

"Kiss me good-bye first." Jace snatched her against him and gave her a quick, hard kiss. "I love you. I'll see you later. Hugh and I are going to try to work the bugs out of Merlin this afternoon."

"Okay. I'll see you later."

When Jace pulled the door open, Rebecca turned and tiptoed out into the hall—directly into the path of her father. For an instant they both froze. Then each jumped back, staring at the other in wide-eyed, open-mouthed shocked.

Hugh stood there in his stocking feet with his shoes dangling from one hand. Muriel stood behind him, her pudgy cheeks as red as ripe tomatoes. She couldn't have looked any guiltier had she been holding a smoking gun in her hand. Rebecca was so stunned, she dropped her sandals. A cat jumped out from behind an umbrella stand and ran away with one.

"Dad!" she exclaimed belatedly.

"Daughter!" Hugh said with a gasp, his face flaming red.

"Oooohhh . . . kitty litter," Muriel muttered, her dimpled hand clutching and unclutching Chester's fur until the gray cat howled a protest and jumped out of her arms.

It was fairly obvious to Rebecca that her father and Muriel Marquardt had spent the night . . . *together*. When she'd told Jace that Hugh and Muriel had fun together, she hadn't realized just what kind of fun. It was Fun, the grown-up kind, the romantic kind. Her father and Muriel the cat lady were having a fling!

Not quite knowing how she should react, Rebecca glanced back over her shoulder. Jace leaned lazily in the doorway of his sitting room with a big grin on his face, obviously finding the situation wildly amusing. He waved to Hugh and Muriel. "Good morning, everyone. How about those Mavericks?"

The Mishawaka Mavericks had to rank among the most hapless teams in the history of the great game of baseball. Other teams set the league championship as their goal for the season. The Mavericks aspired to nothing more than mediocrity. Most people agreed, they set their sights too high.

The Mavericks were a team of has-beens, would-bes, and misfits. Their players were too small, too old, too slow, too green, too weird. They had a left fielder who would have been great except for a nervous condition that made him hyperventilate and pass out along about the sixth inning. They had Pat Wylie, a former big-league catcher whose arm was shot. They had Turk Lacey, who had a smoking fast ball and a talking hand puppet.

The Mavericks were something out of the twilight zone of sport. Their defense had more holes than Swiss cheese. Their team batting average lingered pathetically around a buck ninety-eight. While their neighboring team in South Bend drew legitimate crowds, the Mavericks' fans followed them as a source of comic relief.

Jace was introduced into the lineup in June. With Rebecca keeping a watchful eye on him, he resisted the urge to rush back into the game full force. He knew he risked injuring himself again if he pushed his knee too hard, but he was eager to prove himself. Lacing on his spikes meant his comeback was under way. One of the goals he had set for himself following his accident was within reach, and he wanted to reach for it with all he had.

Rebecca monitored his progress with mixed feelings. The professional in her wanted to help Jace achieve his goal, to bring him back from his injury as quickly as was medically prudent, to keep him in top form so he could return to his former level of play. The woman in her was not so eager for that to happen. She caught herself being overly cautious in his therapy because a part of her didn't want him to go back to baseball. Baseball had taken him away from her once. It would do so again.

Their personal relationship had reached a plateau. They saw each other regularly. They were friends. They were lovers. They had yet to have that talk about the future. Rebecca studiously avoided the topic. She told herself that if Jace made no promises, then neither of them could feel badly if things didn't work out in the end. Somehow the thought didn't offer much comfort.

So they went on in a kind of limbo through the summer. They spent as much time together as their demanding schedules would allow. The Mavericks' road trips often kept them apart for days at a time. When Jace was in town, his free time was divided among Rebecca, Justin, Hugh, and his inventions, and Muriel and the gradual renovation of her house. But for the most part, his focus was on baseball.

Unfortunately for the Mavericks, Jace's intensity was not reflected in their record. One talented, dedicated player couldn't win games when there were eight other guys on the field to mess things up.

"The big question is, can they keep up their record-setting pace?" Dominique asked as the group took their seats in the box Jace had reserved for them along the third-base line. "The Mavericks have a shot at the all-time Class A record for games lost in a season."

"I have complete faith in them," Dr. Cornish announced, adjusting his royal blue cap to cover his growing bald spot.

"Will you listen to that Muriel play?" Hugh said dreamily, as if "Take Me Out to the Ball Game" were a love ballad.

"Mom, look! It's Uncle Jace!" Justin hung over the railing, waving his oversize fielder's glove at Jace.

Jace glanced over, waved, and grinned at them, then turned his attention back to the warm-up routine. He snagged a throw from the first baseman and rifled it to second. Rebecca watched him with respect and awe for his athletic ability. Even with a brace on his knee, his every move was marked by an innate sense of grace and power. And he looked great in pinstripes too.

She shook her head in amazement as she studied his uniform. The team couldn't even manage to get their outfits right. The royal blue logo sewn across the front of their shirts was missing the "s." It read "Maverick." Apparently no one cared enough to fix them.

As the rest of the team straggled toward the dugout, Jace trotted across the warning track toward the stands, his heart swelling in his chest at the sight of Rebecca and Justin waiting for him, smiling at him. Not even knocking Gooden's fastball out of the park in the '88 All-Star game had felt as good.

Rebecca was a vision in a silky salmon-colored tank top and a loose-flowing summer skirt that was white with salmon-colored flowers on it. Justin was adorable with his gap-toothed grin and oversize Mavericks' cap. As he approached the railing, Jace reached up and tugged the boy's cap down over his eyes.

"Hi, sport. Want me to knock one out of the park for you today?"

Justin yanked his cap back up and stared at Jace as if he were Santa Claus. "Would you, Uncle Jace? That would be *so* cool!"

"I'll try." Jace turned and pointed toward the left field fence. "See that sign for the Studebaker Museum? I'll aim for that." He looked up at Rebecca with warm blue eyes. "How about you, beautiful? Anything I can do for you?"

"Come out of the game in one piece," she said, laughing.

"No sweat." He smiled. "I've got the greatest physical therapist in the world, you know."

"Oh, really?"

"Yep. You know what else?" he asked, beckoning her to lean over the railing so he could whisper in her ear. "She's fantastic in the sack too."

The flush that stained Rebecca's cheeks matched the roses blooming in the fabric of her skirt.

"You should have worn a hat," Jace said, teasing. "I think you're getting a sunburn."

He winked at her, waved to the rest of the group in the box, and jogged away.

"I'd turn pink, too, if I had him whispering sweet nothings in my ear," Dominique said, crossing her long, bare legs. She wore a yellow romper that displayed her dark complexion to perfection. A straw hat shaded her exotic face from the afternoon sun.

Rebecca's expression was wistful as she watched Jace join his teammates. Sweet nothings weren't what she wanted to hear from him, and yet she was the one keeping him from saying what her heart longed for.

From the first it was vintage Mavericks baseball. Outfielders collided into one another and dropped fly balls. The second baseman threw a ball into the stands on a double play attempt and beaned a priest. The score was six to nothing at the end of five and a half innings. Jace had gotten two hits but had been left stranded on base both times. The most entertaining part of the game when the Mavericks were at bat was watching their batboy—Merlin the robot.

Jace had dressed Merlin up in a catcher's chest protector and taped a Mavericks' cap to the robot's bubble head. The little machine bustled up to home plate as Jace was warming up in the on-deck circle, shooed the umpire and catcher out of the way, and proceeded to clean the plate with a hand vacuum.

The laughter of the crowd segued into cheers as Jace stepped into the batter's box. He was the team's only bright spot, and he didn't disappoint his followers. He took a two-and-one pitch downtown—popping it over the sign for the Studebaker Museum on the left field fence. As he rounded third base, he grinned and waved to a wildly cheering Justin and Rebecca.

At the top of the sixth, the left fielder started breathing into a paper bag between pitches. He had to be assisted from the field by his hypnotist when he dropped a pop fly, allowing a run to score. Not long after that, Turk Lacey was called in from the bull pen to take over on the pitcher's mound.

After throwing two smoking strikes, he threw three wild pitches—one of which bounced off Merlin, making the robot light up and spin around. The batter warded off the sixth pitch, hitting it in self-defense— right back at Turk. Turk caught the ball, turned, and for no earthly reason fired it to third base, catching Jace a glancing blow off the head.

Rebecca's heart shot to her throat as Jace went down like a felled tree. Before she even realized what she was doing, she was over the railing and running toward him. She pushed her way through the circle of teammates who stood around him, glancing from the groaning Jace to Turk Lacey.

"Jace!" With no regard for her skirt, she knelt in the dirt beside him and pulled his cap off. An angry red abrasion marked the spot where the ball had scraped his temple. Every ounce of medical knowledge she possessed flew out of her head. All she could think of was that she loved him and he was out, cold as a mackerel. What if he never woke up? Tears pooled in her eyes.

"Geez, Spacy," Jerome Tarvin said, peeling off his cap and running his fingers back through his greasy black pompadour, "why'd you have to go and bean the only decent player we've got?"

Turk's bushy mustache twitched worriedly beneath his goose-beak nose.

The team's manager joined the group as Dr. Cornish knelt by Jace. "Is he okay, Doc?"

"I don't know." Dr. Cornish took Jace's pulse and lifted one eyelid to check the response of his pupil to light. "Jace? Jace, can you hear me?"

Jace opened his eyes but couldn't quite focus them as he looked at the doctor. "Would that I were a glove upon thine hand that I might touch thy cheek," he recited in stilted tones. "Did I get all the words right this time, Mrs. Brutworg?"

Dr. Cornish looked up at the manager. "He's been knocked silly."

Rebecca bit her lip and stroked Jace's hair. "Jace, sweetheart, it's me, Becca."

"Becca." He smiled inanely as he continued staring at Dr. Cornish. "Will you go to the prom with me?"

Tears spilled down her cheeks as they helped him up and walked him to the dugout and down the hall to the locker room.

'I'm all right," Jace protested as he took a seat on a rubbing table in the trainer's room, which was located between the locker area and the showers. He shook his head to clear it, then winced and cradled it in his hands as it began to throb.

"Where are you?" Dr. Cornish asked calmly as he checked Jace's reflexes.

"The locker room in Mishawaka."

"Who are you?"

"Jace Cooper."

"Do you think the Kings will have a decent shot at the pennant?"

"Well—"

"Stop it!" Rebecca shrieked.

Both men turned to stare at her, stunned right down to their socks. Rebecca never shrieked. She couldn't remember ever having a totally irrational moment in her life. Well, she was having one now.

She threw a wet towel at Dr. Cornish. "How can you ask such a stupid question when Jace could have a concussion? What's the matter with you?"

"Nothing. Rebecca, he's going to be just fine." The doctor spoke to her slowly and carefully, as if he thought she were dangerously unbalanced and would go stark raving mad at the slightest provocation. "There's no sign of a concussion."

Jace motioned Dr. Cornish toward the door as Rebecca started crying in earnest. The doctor shrugged and beat a hasty retreat.

Easing himself off the table, Jace took Rebecca gently in his arms. She buried her nose against the shoulder of his dusty uniform and sobbed.

"You scared me half to death!"

"I'm sorry, honey," Jace said sincerely. He stroked her ebony hair and offered her comfort.

"Why'd I have to go and fall in love with *you*?" she asked angrily. "You make me crazy. I'm *never* crazy."

"No, sweetheart," Jace murmured, kissing her ear, "you're never crazy."

"Why'd I have to fall for a man with such a dangerous occupation?"

"Baseball isn't dangerous, honey. This was a freak accident."

She scowled up at him. "This *team* is a freak accident."

"You'll get no argument about that," Jace said. "With any luck, I won't be playing with this team much longer."

Rebecca let her head fall back onto his shoulder again. For a long moment she didn't say anything, just leaned against him, listening to the showers dripping in the next room. When she did speak, it was a truth she hadn't wanted to reveal to him.

"I don't want that either," she said softly.

Jace moved back a step and stared at her, feeling betrayed. "You don't want me to go back to the Kings?"

"I want you to succeed, Jace. I really do. But part of me is so afraid I'm going to lose you. I'm afraid that once you go back to Chicago, you'll forget about me." She let her gaze drop to the royal blue pinstripes on his shirt and the logo with the missing "s." "I don't know if I could go through that again, Jace."

"Look at me, Becca." When she didn't raise her head, he gave her a shake. Startled, she stared into his eyes. "There's no way you're going to lose me. I love you. I'd marry you tomorrow if it weren't for the season and my career being up in the air and the fact that I don't have a penny to my name. Say the word, and we'll get engaged right here and now."

But Rebecca couldn't say the word. It was stuck in her throat. Jace was offering to make a promise, and experience had taught her he wasn't terribly good at keeping them.

"What do you want, Becca?" he asked tiredly.

Everything. Nothing. She closed her eyes against the confusion. She hadn't had a moment's peace since he'd come back to Mishawaka. Her heart hadn't had a moment's rest since he'd left seven years ago.

"Just hold me," she whispered as tears squeezed between her thick black lashes and streamed down her cheeks.

Jace cursed himself. What kind of man was he, pushing her when she was feeling frightened and vulnerable? A frightened and vulnerable man, he supposed.

He held her for a time, savoring the feel of her in his arms. She felt so right there. She fit against him perfectly, like the piece that had been missing from the puzzle of his life for a long, long time. She was afraid of losing him? The thought of going back to the life he'd had without her terrified him.

He wouldn't lose her. He wouldn't let that happen now that he was so close to having it all. He had nearly thrown his life away once. Now he'd wrestled every demon he had and put his life back on track, never to be derailed again.

He only wished Rebecca would see that and believe in him.

"I'm sorry I fell apart on you like that," she said, lifting her head from his shoulder.

Jace gave her a gentle smile. "Hey, it's okay. Even you are entitled to get a little wacky every once in a while, Miss Levelheaded. I'm flattered you went wacky over me."

Rebecca sniffled and chuckled and reached a hand up to brush his smoky blond hair away from the welt on his head. "Speaking of wacky—are you sure you're okay?"

"I'm going to have a doozy of a headache, but I promise I'm not going to start talking with a hand puppet or anything like that."

"Good." Her eyes flooded again as she murmured, "I love you."

"I know." He also knew the prospect didn't exactly thrill her, but he silently promised her that would change. He was winning all the other battles he'd begun after that horrible night on the expressway in Chicago. He would win this one too.

"Hey," Jace said, glancing around at the shabby trainer's room, a mischievous smile twitching his lips as his spirit lightened, "ever do it in a locker room?"

"Jace Cooper!" Rebecca said with a gasp, her heart pounding as he backed her toward the rubbing table. "Are you crazy?"

"Yep. Crazy for you." His hands worked her salmon-colored tank top up out of the waistband of her flowered skirt as he nibbled on her neck. "How about it? Feel like a quickie?"

The very idea seemed so illicit, it thrilled her. Rebecca had never been the Bradshaw girl who got caught smoking in the restroom at school or fooling around with her boyfriend under the bleachers in the gym. It occurred to her that it might be a lot of fun to do something she would ordinarily have considered forbidden. And Jace was just the man to do it with. He had always been the adventuresome one. He had given her a taste of that kind of fun a long time ago. Now he was offering to again. She tried to look disapproving, however. "I think that beanball scrambled your brain.

Maybe we ought to take you in to the hospital for a CAT scan."

"I can assure you, I am in full possession of my faculties." He waggled his dark eyebrows lasciviously as he leaned into her. "And everything else is in working order too. Wanna see?"

Rebecca glanced from the closed door back to Jace. Nibbling on her lower lip, she whispered, "Maybe."

The Mavericks lost the game ten to three. Meanwhile, the score in the locker room was a tie—both players went home with smiles on their faces.

Nine

It was Sunday. It was raining. Rebecca couldn't have been happier. The Mavericks had been scheduled for an afternoon home game against Kenosha, but the ballpark would be empty. No game would be played today. She glanced out the window at the steady shower and smiled.

Justin, Hugh, and Muriel were spending the afternoon together, going first to a Disney double feature and then to Captain Jack's for pizza and video games. Rebecca had begged off, saying she had too much paperwork to catch up on.

That was a fib. The paperwork was going to stay where it was on her desk in the study. She had every intention of spending the afternoon with her attention focused on Jace. She hadn't seen him in ten days. The team had been on a road trip, and the night they had returned Rebecca had been tied up in yet another hospital board meeting. Their schedules would have kept them apart for another few days if it hadn't been for the rain.

She moved around her room lighting candles and turning down the covers on the bed. As she waited for the ring of the doorbell, she focused her attention on arranging the fresh fruit and croissants on the small table she had set up beside her window.

Suddenly bleeps and buzzes drew Rebecca's attention to the door. Merlin rolled in holding a black lacquered tray in front of him. On the tray was a small bouquet of blue delphinium and a bottle of sparkling apple cider. Laughing, she accepted the tray the robot offered and put it down on the table with the rest of the brunch she had prepared. When she turned around, the machine lit up with a blaze of blinking multicolored lights. It bleeped at her and advanced on her, accordion arms outstretched as if to embrace her.

"No, Merlin," Rebecca ordered, backing away from the robot. It just kept coming, rolling smoothly across the blue carpet. Rebecca scooted backward, trying to keep out of reach of Merlin's metal claw hands. "Stop. Merlin, heel. Merlin? Merlin! Aargh!"

Jace rushed in, remote control in hand, just as Rebecca tumbled backward across the bed. "Merlin!"

'Merlin?" she questioned indignantly, raking her black hair back out of her eyes. "What about me?"

"You may be one of a kind, sweetheart," Jace said as he opened a door in Merlin's back and performed some quick surgery, "but Merlin is a prototype."

"Gee, thanks," she muttered dryly. The robot's lights went off, and it seemed to sigh and go limp as its power shut down. "I thought you had all the bugs worked out of that mechanical malcontent."

"We do. Merlin's been running like a top. It must be you."

"Me! I didn't ask to be assaulted by that computer-run Casanova."

Jace scratched his head, bemused. "He always seems

to go haywire around you. I think you must have a weird magnetic field around you or something."

He snapped the robot's door shut and flopped down on the bed beside Rebecca. His eyes glowed like lapis lazuli as he gave her a warm smile. "You certainly attract me."

She groaned at his pun but accepted his kiss, amazed at the wild thrill that still shot through her at his touch.

"Hi," he murmured, brushing her hair back from her cheek with his fingertips.

"Hi," she whispered.

"I missed you."

"I missed you. How did you get in? The doors were locked."

"I bypassed Hugh's security system. No sweat."

Rebecca made a face. "I can't even get in with a key."

"I guess I just have magic fingers," Jace said, drawing the tips of those magic fingers down the slender white column of her throat. He purred in appreciation at the shiver that went through her.

"I won't argue with that," Rebecca murmured, arching into his touch. "I can't come up with a more logical explanation of the effect you have on me."

As she angled her head to meet his kiss, Rebecca caught a glimpse of Merlin standing beside the bed, seemingly staring down at them with the little wire gizmos in his clear bubble head. Jace's kiss glanced off her chin as she stared back at the robot.

"Um, Jace? Can you roll him out into the hall or something? I'd rather not have an audience."

"Honey," Jace said, groaning in frustration, "he's a machine. He—unlike myself—isn't even turned on at the moment."

Rebecca's mouth dropped into a sultry pout as she glared at the robot. "Just the same . . ."

"Think of him as a vacuum cleaner."

"Vacuum cleaners don't stare."

Jace chuckled as he rolled onto his back and scooped up the remote control he'd tossed onto the bed. Punching a few buttons, he brought Merlin to life and directed the robot out to the hall, even getting the machine to close the door behind it.

"There," he said, placing the remote on the nightstand. "Satisfied?"

Rebecca sighed and smiled at him, feeling a ridiculous sense of relief. "Yes."

Jace lowered himself beside her on the bed. "Well, I'm not."

Growling playfully, he rolled across the bed with Rebecca in his arms, nibbling at her neck, tickling her ribs. Then he settled himself gently on top of her and gave her a long, thorough kiss to make up for all the kisses they'd missed out on while he'd been away. Thoroughly he explored the shape and texture of her lips. Leisurely he dipped his tongue into the dark warmth of her mouth, savoring the taste of her, inviting her to taste him as well. When he finally raised his head a fraction of an inch, they were both smiling like cats sated after a bowl of cream.

"How've you been?" he asked softly against her lips. "Besides unbearably lonely for me?"

"Fine."

"How's Justin?"

"Enjoying Sparky," she said, referring to the mechanical dog Jace had built. "He says Sparky is almost better than a real dog because he doesn't get fleas."

Jace's heart warmed at the thought that he had made the boy happy. He could hardly wait for the day Justin would call him Dad instead of Uncle Jace. It was amazing how one freckle-faced six-year-old could bring out paternal feelings he hadn't even realized he had.

"How've you been?" Rebecca asked. "How's the knee?"

"It's been fine. Great, actually. No problem on defense or running the bases. The team lost five of seven games, but I'm batting three-fifteen. My agent tells me he's hearing rumors from the Kings' management. They've got a tough schedule going down the stretch for the division championship . . ."

A chill ran through her heart as Rebecca listened to Jace's talk of the major league. She'd been following the reports of the last Mavericks' road trip in the sports section, reading every glowing account of Jace's play. To hear him talk about it himself, to hear the excitement in his voice when he spoke of the possibility of moving back to the majors, made it even more real to her—Jace wouldn't be with the Mavericks forever.

According to the local experts, there was no question —he would be going back to Chicago as the Kings made a bid for the division championship. Back to Chicago and the environment that had tempted him nearly to ruin his life, back to the way of life that had taken him from her seven years ago.

No, Rebecca told herself, that was in the future, and she had promised herself nothing would intrude on their afternoon together. She forced a smile and pressed a finger to Jace's lips. "Enough shop talk for now. I've fixed us this wonderful brunch, and frankly I'm starved."

"Me too," Jace said seriously, lowering his mouth toward hers. "I'm so hungry for you, I can't think straight."

There had been a time when he had enjoyed road trips, seeing new sights and new faces. But travel had lost its appeal. With each trip his longing to come home—home to Rebecca and Justin—grew stronger. On each trip the nights seemed longer as he lay awake aching to hold the woman he loved.

Brunch was forgotten as Jace's hands freed the buttons on Rebecca's emerald green blouse. He opened the garment, then dealt with the front hook of her lacy white bra, baring her breasts to his reverent gaze. Her breath stilled in her lungs as his mouth tenderly closed over one taut peak.

It seemed it had been forever since he'd last touched her. Her body craved his as a flower craves light and water. She felt herself coming to life under his hands and mouth, as if she had lain dormant in his absence. Heat and electricity surged under the surface of her hypersensitive skin as he undressed her.

As eager to please as to be pleased, Rebecca returned the favor, ridding Jace of his shirt and running her hands over the hard, athletic body she loved. Willingly she gave in to her desire, shutting out everything but the man and the moment. As they kneeled together on the bed, she dragged her lips across his chest, kissing and tasting, flicking her tongue across the tightly knotted flesh of his nipples.

Jace groaned and reached between them, freeing himself from his jeans and briefs. He sighed as his most sensitive flesh pressed against Rebecca's softness. Then her hand closed around him, stroking, teasing, tempting him, guiding him. She slipped him between her legs and moved against him, inviting him to take the final step to unite them in an act of love as old as time.

"Becca, I love you," he whispered as he lowered them both to the mattress and eased himself into her welcoming warmth.

Rebecca arched to meet his thrust, the words of love she felt for him so deeply embedded in her soul, she couldn't speak them, she could only feel them. She sought to let Jace feel them as well, through her movements, through her touch. She reached out to him, bound herself to him on a plane where no words existed.

Their loving seemed to last forever. And when the end

came, it went on and on, carrying them both on a wave of bliss. Then they floated down gently from the incredible height their love had taken them to. For a long time they were content to lie in each other's arms, silent and complete as they listened to the rain.

"How about that brunch?" Rebecca asked as she slid out of bed and slipped into Jace's shirt. It fell to the tops of her thighs. She smiled sleepily as she flipped the collar up and caught Jace's clean, masculine scent clinging to the fabric.

Jace got up and pulled his jeans on. His attention was on Rebecca. His heart was in his throat. "How about we get engaged?"

Rebecca's hand stopped on the bottle of apple cider. Outwardly she appeared calm, but inside her was a riot of emotion, fear the chief among them. It seemed that the much-dreaded discussion of their future was at hand, and she had the sinking feeling Jace would not be sidetracked this time.

Toying with the cork in the cider bottle, she said evenly, "I thought you needed to concentrate on your game right now."

Jace didn't realize he'd been holding his breath until it began to burn in his lungs. He sighed and fleetingly wished for a cigarette. Somehow he had known Rebecca wouldn't be overjoyed by his suggestion. Just the same, her reaction—or lack of it—hurt. He tried to push the hurt aside as he answered her.

"I'll be able to concentrate better knowing you're here waiting for me."

She didn't turn to face him but bowed her head as if in defeat. Her gaze rested on the delicate blue flowers he had sent her, so pretty, so fragile. "You know I'll always be here waiting for you, Jace."

Her voice was low and heavy with resignation, telling him she wasn't pleased with the realization she had finally come to face. Anger simmered deep inside him. Dammit, was it such a terrible hardship for her to love him? Did she really have to make it sound like a life sentence in prison with no hope of parole?

"You'll be here waiting," he said tightly, "but you don't know that I'll always come back. Is that it?"

That was it in a nutshell, Rebecca thought. Guilt and shame lashed out inside her like twin whips. Jace had tried so hard to change. She had seen the effort and the results, but she couldn't shake the fear that the changes were in part a knee-jerk reaction to his accident and his own guilt over what had happened to Casey Mercer. Time would tell, but Jace was asking her to cut that time to nothing.

She turned to face him, almost wincing at the accusation in his eyes. "I just think you have enough pressure on you right now without making promises to me as well."

"Promises you don't believe I'll keep," he said angrily. He jammed one hand on his bare waist, just above his low-riding jeans, and raked the other back through his tousled hair. "Dammit, Rebecca, what do I have to do to prove myself to you? I've changed. I've shown you how. I've shown you why. How many more hoops do I have to jump through?"

"I know you've changed. I know why. I admire your loyalty to Casey, Jace, but I don't want to wonder if I'm part of your penance."

"What the hell is that supposed to mean?"

She squeezed her eyes shut and whispered, "Nothing."

"No," he insisted, his jaw set at a belligerent angle. "You're the one with the two-twenty IQ and the college education. Explain it to me."

Rebecca took a deep breath and let it out slowly. She

could explain it until she was blue in the face, and he wouldn't listen, not when he was feeling hurt and defensive. "You've had a terrible experience, you're reacting to it. You told me something good had to come out of what happened to Casey. Maybe right now you think that something is marriage and a family."

His opinion of her theory came out in a stream of muttered curses. "That ridiculous. I love you, Becca. Just because my priorities changed after the accident doesn't make them false."

"I didn't say they were false. I just think you should give yourself some time. You've taken yourself out of the environment that put so much pressure on you, you almost ruined your life. What happens when you go back? You'll have more demands on you than ever before, Jace. Not only the demands of the game and celebrity status, but demands you'll put on yourself as well."

He began pacing beside the unmade bed, his bare feet padding softly across the blue rug. He wanted to hit something or run, but the time for running was over. Deep in his gut was that bottom-of-the-ninth feeling, that two-outs-and-two-strikes feeling. Reining in his fears, he stopped and faced Rebecca.

"You think I'll knuckle under?" he asked coolly. One dark eyebrow stretched upward in a sardonic question. "You think I'll get back to Chicago, pop a few brewskies, and race out to the track to blow my paycheck on the horses?"

Rebecca rubbed a hand across her suddenly aching forehead. She wasn't trying to undermine his confidence. She only wanted to make him see the need for caution. And, yes, dammit, she wanted to protect herself.

"I just—" She stopped and shook her head, frustration rubbing her nerves raw. "I don't want promises from you now, Jace."

He closed the distance between them with three angry strides. When he spoke again, his face was only inches from hers, close enough so Rebecca could see the pain and the fury in it. "Well, maybe you don't want promises, but I *need* to make them, Becca. Can you understand that? I *need* to promise you I'll come back. I *need* to have you believe me. You want some kind of proof I'll come back. I'm offering it now. You're the one who's not willing to make a commitment to this relationship, Rebecca."

He backed off a yard and began pacing again, his gaze riveted to the floor. His voice vibrated with barely restrained emotion. "If you had any idea of the hell I've gone through trying to start my whole stinking life over, then you'd understand that I could use a little support. I don't think it's asking too much to want the woman I love to have a little faith in me."

"I do—"

He stopped and shot her a look so incredulous, it cut her to the quick. "No, you don't. I know I hurt you once. That was seven years ago, Rebecca. We were hardly more than kids. I admit I made a mistake. How long am I going to have to pay for it? You were the judge and the jury. Tell me what the sentence is for making a mistake?"

The sharp sense of *déjà vu* was like being poked with a needle. Her sister had used almost those same words seven years ago when they'd fought about Ellen's lack of responsibility. Rebecca tried to tell herself she wasn't still passing judgment on Jace, she was only being careful.

"What's the matter, Becca? Doesn't your logical, practical mind have a list of guidelines for offenses?" he asked sarcastically. "Do I get credit for time already served? Does it matter that I love you, that I want to have a life with you? Or are you going to hold it over my head for the rest of my life that I wasn't always as mature and responsible as you?"

"I'm not holding it over your head," she denied softly, staring down at her clasped hands as tears rose in her eyes.

Jace's laugh was nothing more than derision. "The hell you're not."

"You say that as if I don't have a right to!" she shouted, glaring at him. "You broke my heart! That may be a 'little mistake' to you, but it's a lot more than that to me. Do you have any idea how long I hurt after you left?"

A measure of control came back to her as her question hung in the air between them. She turned to one side, combing her hair back with a trembling hand. "Yes, I'm afraid of it happening again. I don't think I could live through it."

"You won't have to," Jace said quietly. He had never meant for this to escalate into a fight. The last thing he wanted to do was drag up the past and hurt Rebecca. He wanted the past behind them, but it seemed he couldn't quite close the door on it. She wouldn't let him. "Trust me, Rebecca. Let me make that promise."

It was a simple statement, and yet he was asking too much. Jace saw his promise as a tie that would bind him to her even in his absence. Rebecca saw it as a string that could easily be broken once he had his career back on track. It was a difference of perspective, she thought sadly, one that wasn't going to be resolved. Why couldn't he just have left the future alone? They could have gone on drifting with no promises to keep or to break.

A weary sigh ribboned out of her. "They haven't called you back yet. We could be arguing for no reason."

"No, Becca," Jace said sadly. "Believing in me can't be conditional. I have to have your trust whether I stay here or go back to the Kings. Love can't have those kinds of restrictions put on it and still be called love. It may not be logical for you to trust me, but you can't love me without doing it."

The silence was thick around them as Jace waited for Rebecca to make some kind of comment. The only sound that same was that of rain on the window and a distant rumble of thunder.

"Maybe you don't love me. Maybe I'm the one who's being a fool."

Rebecca's troubled gaze met his as she hurried to reassure him. "I do love you, Jace, but—"

"No. No qualification, no proviso. Either you love me, you believe in me, or you don't. Maybe you ought to take a little time to think about that," he said, going to the door. He stopped with his hand on the doorknob and turned to look back at Rebecca. "Let me know when you decide you're willing to take a chance on me. I'll be around. That's a promise, Becca."

Rebecca closed her eyes rather than watch him walk out. Pain swelled and surged inside her like a flood tide. She wanted to call him back, but the words wouldn't form. When she heard the muted sound of the back door closing, she opened her eyes and stared out at the rain-washed backyard, watching as Jace walked slowly toward the brown house across the alley, shirtless, with his hands jammed in the pockets of his worn jeans. Then he disappeared through the back door, leaving three orange cats sitting forlornly on the porch.

He was gone. The emptiness inside her was a cold, hollow ache. Shivering, she pulled his shirt closer around her and wept.

Ten

The words of the article on hydrotherapy blurred in front of her yet again. Rebecca sat back in her desk chair, pulled her glasses off, and rubbed her eyes with no regard for what was left of her eye makeup. Her desk top was nearly covered by stacks of files and patient reports. One whole side of the thing was devoted to information on the proposed expansion of the physical therapy department.

Griffith Saunders had promised her he would use the muscle he had as head administrator to get the board to make a final decision this month. Rebecca was to meet with him again that afternoon to discuss options. She should have been arming herself with information for a final campaign to get the improvements she felt they needed, but she couldn't concentrate.

All she could think of was Jace. She hadn't seen him in days. She missed him. He was still spending time with Justin and Hugh, but he managed to avoid running into her. She supposed he was being true to his word, giving her time to think, but thinking was taking a backseat to missing and hurting.

It seemed the separation was having its affects on Jace as well. Her father hadn't actually come right out and told her so, but he had given her plenty of none-too-subtle hints. Grumbling under his breath while his white mustache twitched was a classic sign of Hugh being out of sorts with somebody. The sharp looks he gave Rebecca told her she was the one in his doghouse.

Just that morning at breakfast he had come up with a comment that might have seemed out of the blue if his feelings toward Jace hadn't been so clear. "For someone so intelligent, you can be awfully stupid."

When Rebecca had asked for an explanation of that statement, all she'd gotten was more grumbling and mustache twitching. As raw as her feelings were these days, that was as bad as a lecture.

Justin had delivered the double whammy when he entered the kitchen pouting because Rebecca had told him the night before that their planned Saturday outing to the Hannah Lindahl Children's Museum was not going to include Jace.

He had stared at her with hurt and anger in his fathomless blue eyes, a frown tugging his freckles down. "We never get to do stuff together with Uncle Jace anymore. How come you're being so mean?"

"I'm not trying to be mean, honey—"

"You are so! I wanted Uncle Jace to be my dad, and now you're making him stay away!"

Things had gone downhill from there. Thinking about it now, Rebecca couldn't stop feeling a surge of resentment toward Jace. One of the things she had feared most in having him around was having Justin become too attached to him, only to be disappointed when the end of the relationship came. That was exactly what was happening.

But it wasn't really Jace's fault, was it? The voice of truth and justice asked inside her. Because she had never been much of a liar, she had to answer truthfully. No. For the time being, she was the one to blame. Jace hadn't left Mishawaka—yet. He hadn't broken any promises—yet.

Jace couldn't see she was doing him a favor by not letting him make promises to her before he got called back to Chicago. Rebecca didn't want to add to the pressure that would be on him. And, adding that annoying little troubadour of truth, she didn't want to add to her hopes, because she knew from experience that the higher they were, the more pain she would suffer when they were crushed beneath the hobnailed boot of reality.

Now she swiveled absently back and forth in her desk chair, second-guessing herself. Was Jace asking too much, or was she simply willing to give too little? Was she still punishing him for not being the perfect All-American star? Was she still punishing him for breaking her heart?

Everyone made mistakes; most deserved to be forgiven. She was willing to forgive him, but her heart wasn't able to forget. It kept whispering inside her— what if? What if she trusted Jace and he let her down again?

What if she didn't trust him?

The question trailed away to thoughts of the past weeks. Rebecca looked out the window of her office to the exercise room. Jace had worked so hard to come back from his injury, without complaint, without bitterness for what had happened to him. He had helped and encouraged other patients as well. He hadn't been the spoiled star. He hadn't been the slick, smiling con man who had charmed her into going out with him seven years before. His concern and compassion had been genuine.

As it had been when he'd held her the night she'd

told him about Justin's parentage. He had been so understanding, so caring.

She recalled all the time he'd spent with Justin, time that hadn't diminished after he'd found out the boy wasn't his son. She thought of all the patient lessons on how to play baseball. She thought of the mechanical dog Jace had built to soothe Justin's disappointment at not being able to have a real pet.

She closed her eyes and brought back that night in the parking lot at Captain Jack's. She could still hear the strain in his voice when he told her he hadn't had a drink in four months. She could still see the vulnerability, the fear, and the determination not to give in to it.

And she could picture him standing over Casey Mercer in his hospital bed—hurting, blaming himself, punishing himself. She could still hear the anguish in his voice when he'd said he'd never meant to hurt anybody. She could still feel his tears on her shoulder.

The Jace Cooper she'd known so long ago wouldn't have owned up to faults or mistakes or accepted responsibility for what had happened because a young teammate had idolized the wrong aspects of a hero. Jace had grown and matured. He had fought hard to change. She was being unfair to him in believing the changes were only temporary. It was natural for her to want to protect herself, but she was hurting Jace in the process. The changes he had made in his life had been made over a long, hard road, one he was still struggling over—alone.

Is it too much to ask that the woman I love have a little faith in me?

If he went back to Chicago, the pressure put on him would be intense. Fans, friends, and the press would be expecting the old Jace—the party boy, the high roller, the star. Team management would have him under a microscope, demanding perfection and yet waiting for him to make a mistake. Everyone would be watching every move he made.

And he would be alone.

He needed her support. He needed her love. He needed her friendship.

"Someone dropped this at the nurses' station for you," Dominique said as she walked into Rebecca's office. Taking the seat across the desk from her friend, she handed Rebecca an envelope with her name scribbled on the front of it.

There was no note, just a snapshot. Rebecca let the envelope fall to her desk as she stared at the picture. The photo was of a stream and trees and a meadow at sunset. It might have been taken the day before or years before—there was no way of telling. Perhaps it was that sense of timelessness that struck her most about the picture. It was a place everyday life could not intrude upon, a place made for memories. And the memories flowed unchecked through Rebecca's mind and heart.

In this place an uncertain girl had confided in the only person who had ever understood her. In this place friendship had taken root. In this place she had fallen in love. In this place she had become a woman. In this place, just weeks ago, love had struggled to bloom anew.

Rebecca's hand began to tremble, and she turned the photograph over to put it down. On the back was written a verse she recognized as being from the Bible.

Love bears all things, believes all things, endures all things.

"It looks like a very special place," Dominique said softly.

Not trusting her voice, Rebecca nodded. It was a very special place she had shared with a very special friend—a special friend who was asking her to believe in him.

"I do love him," she whispered, fighting back tears.

"I know." Dominique gave her a sad little smile as she unfolded her long frame, standing and moving toward the open door. The light in her ebony eyes was one of empathy. "That's not always the easiest thing, is it?"

No, Rebecca thought as she watched her friend leave, sometimes there wasn't anything easy about love. It could be the simplest of emotions or the most complex. The risks involved could be enormous, the rewards unimaginably wonderful—and you couldn't win one without chancing the other.

A heart once broken could be a selfish, suspicious thing. But Jace was right, there could be no conditions, no restrictions on love. She had to be willing to believe in him wholeheartedly. She had to be willing to put her heart in his hands, or the love she professed for him meant nothing.

He was the only man she'd ever loved. He was the only man she would ever love so intensely. He was the only man who had ever made her feel so complete as a woman. He was the only person who knew her soul deep.

Staring out the window, she watched Dominique explain the fine art of negotiating steps on crutches to a weekend warrior who had broken his ankle playing soccer. Bob Wilkes was working out on the weight machine. His face was shiny with sweat and tense with concentration. Because her door stood open, Rebecca could hear the squeak and sigh of the machine as Bob worked.

Suddenly he stopped his routine and yanked off the earphones to the portable radio he was wearing. "Hey, everybody! Super Cooper's been called up to Chicago! It was just on the radio. He's supposed to join the team today!"

As a cheer went up from the small crowd in the PT room, Rebecca bolted up in her chair and grabbed the phone on her desk. Frantically, she punched Muriel's number. She had to catch Jace before he left. She had to tell him she'd come to a decision. But the phone on the other end of the line rang unanswered. A call to her own house was no more successful. Grabbing her purse and the snapshot from her desk top, she dashed out of her office.

"Dominique," she shouted, "you have to cover for me, please. I have to go."

Dominique looked shocked to the ends of her wild black mane, probably because Rebecca never asked anyone to cover for her. "What about your meeting with Mr. Saunders?"

"It'll have to wait," Rebecca said as she headed for the door. "This is more important."

Her friend's mouth curved upward in a knowing smile. "Good luck."

Everywhere Rebecca went, it seemed as though she was one step behind Jace. No one she talked to seemed to know exactly where he was—until she ran into Turk Lacey at the ballpark. Turk was his usual recalcitrant self, but Mr. Peppy, the hand puppet, told her Jace had gone to the bus depot.

As she drove to the other side of town, Rebecca cursed speed limits, bad timing, and herself. Why had it taken her so blasted long to see what should have been plain to her all along? The part of Jace Cooper that had made him capable of hurting her seven years ago no longer existed! The sharp edges and slick shine of his youth had been worn down by time and hard lessons, leaving all the qualities she had fallen in love with intact. The Jace Cooper who had come back to Mishawaka was a good man, a kind man. He was a man who had made mistakes but was well worth forgiving . . . and supporting . . . and loving.

As she sat waiting impatiently at a red light, Rebecca felt a sense of panic that cut her to the core. She had to catch Jace before he left. She had to tell him before he went back to Chicago that she loved him and believed in him.

In the parking lot of the bus depot she parked her Honda, then fumbled trying to get her keys out of the ignition. She left them, deciding she would rather have her car stolen than miss catching Jace. Running across the asphalt, she broke the heel of one of her black pumps, but it hardly slowed her down.

Inside the building her eyes scanned the small crowd. There was no sign of Jace. An elderly woman sat knitting on one of the green plastic chairs. Several seats down a young mother fanned herself and her sleeping baby with a magazine. There were some rough-looking characters hanging around an old cigarette machine, and two teenage boys with duffel bags resting at their feet were playing a video game. There was no sign of Jace.

Rebecca's heart pounded in her chest like a gong. She'd missed him. To confirm her fears, she asked the man behind the ticket window about the bus schedule to Chicago. He informed her that a bus had gone at two-thirty and the next didn't leave until six-fifteen. She'd missed him by no more than five minutes.

Now she knew how balloons felt when they were suddenly deflated, Rebecca thought as she drove slowly home. Tears trickled down her cheeks, but she paid no attention to them. She felt hollow and shriveled up inside—guilty because she hadn't gone to Jace sooner, hurt because he hadn't come to say good-bye.

Wearing one shoe with a heel and one without, Rebecca limped to the back door of her home. It didn't surprise her in the least that she couldn't get into the house. No one seemed to be home, and Hugh's security system flatly refused to let her in, beeping at her angrily as she tried repeatedly to punch in the code she had memorized.

When she finally sat down on the step to cry, she felt like a complete and utter failure. Not only had she blown her chance with Jace, she couldn't even manage to get inside her own house. Her father was angry with her, her son thought she was mean. She was neglecting her duties at the hospital, and she had ruined her best pair of shoes.

Sniffling, she leaned back against the locked door, drew her knees up, and arranged the skirt of her dress. Then she dug through her purses and pulled out the photograph Jace had sent her.

Love bears all things, believes all things, endures all things.

Maybe this had been his way of saying good-bye and telling her to remember him and to remember all the wonderful things they had shared. Or maybe he had meant it was a reminder of all the things she was turning her back on by not trusting him. Either way, just looking at the beautiful, peaceful scene made her ache with misery and longing and regret.

Her logic and intellect had gotten her nowhere. The high standards of conduct she had imposed on everyone had left her nothing but lonely. Now that it was too late, she realized love meant forgiveness and trust.

Her father's words came back to her, more bitter when delivered by her own inner voice. *For someone so intelligent, you can be awfully stupid.*

Giving in to the need to feel sorry for herself, Rebecca crossed her arms over her drawn-up knees, put her head down, and sobbed. But even as she sobbed, her brain was making plans. She would have to go to Chicago and find Jace. If he wanted her to, she would stay with him. That would mean turning her patients over to Dominique and Max. She would have to take a leave of absence. She had responsibilities at the hospital, but they weren't as important to her as her responsibilities to the man she loved. Jace needed her now.

She only hoped he would still want her, because she knew she would never feel complete without him.

"Becca?" a soft voice questioned. "Honey, don't cry. I'll let you in the house."

Rebecca looked up, her watery gaze landing on Jace. Through her tears his image shimmered like a mirage. "Jace! What are you doing here?"

"I came to let you in," he said. "I saw you from my window. Don't feel bad, honey. Not everyone is mechanical."

Pushing herself to her feet, she swiped at the tears that clung to her thick black lashes. "No," she said in a voice rusty from crying. "I meant that I thought you'd left for Chicago. Turk sent me to the bus depot, but when I got there you were gone."

Jace felt his insides go tense with anticipation. "Is that why you were crying?"

"Yes," she whispered. And now she felt like crying again. Tears of relief brimmed and teetered on her eyelids. It wasn't too late. She could still tell Jace how she felt about him—provided he wanted to hear it.

"I went to the depot to see Jerome Tarvin off," Jace said. He went to the door and successfully operated the security system, opening the door as the green light on the box beamed and Rebecca's recorded voice invited him inside. "He got a full-time job as an Elvis impersonator in Reno."

"How nice for him," Rebecca murmured politely.

"Yeah," Jace said, turning to face her once again. "He was a lousy shortstop, but he does a great Elvis."

An awkward silence fell between them. Jace looked down and gently plucked the photograph from Rebecca's fingers. He looked from it to her, waiting for her to say something, anything.

Rebecca took a deep breath and tried to swallow down the knot of fear in her throat. Once she dredged up the courage she needed, she decided not to mince words. She looked Jace square in the eye and said, "I love you. I believe in you."

Tears of emotion flooded her eyes and her voice nearly failed her, but she went on, desperately needing to tell him what was in her heart, and even more desperately needing him to accept it. "I am so proud of you, of the way you've taken charge of your life, of the way you've fought to change. I never should have doubted you, Jace, but I was so afraid of getting hurt again."

"You're not afraid anymore?" he asked evenly.

A shiver chased over her skin even though it was a hot afternoon. Jace's expression was guarded as he waited for her answer. The breeze ruffled his hair and swirled Rebecca's skirt around her legs.

"Yes," she said honestly. "I'm afraid. Afraid you won't forgive me."

For a moment Jace just stood there, afraid to move. If he moved, maybe he would break the spell and wake up alone in his bed and realize Rebecca's words had been nothing more than a dream. When she reached out to touch his arm, his breath left him on a long sigh of relief. She was real, this was real.

Pulling her to him, he wrapped his arms around her and held her close, burying his nose in the elegant silk of her dark hair. He had missed her so badly since their fight, he had literally ached to hold her. He had lain awake at night wondering if he would ever be able to hold her again or if she would ever let go of their past long enough to see they could have a future together. Now he savored the contact of her body nestling against his. He pressed his lips to her cheek, breathing deeply of her soft, sweet fragrance.

"Go to Chicago and knock 'em dead," Rebecca murmured, pressing her head against his shoulder. "I'll be rooting for you."

"Umm . . . about that . . ." Jace pulled back a little and gave her a sheepish look. "I'm not going."

Rebecca's face dropped. "What?"

Jace shrugged in apology. He felt kind of foolish telling her this now that she'd poured her heart out in a big admission of love and trust. "I'm not going."

"But they called you. It was on the radio," she said.

"I know. They did call me this morning," he said. "But I've given it a lot of thought and decided you're more important to me than a second chance at stardom. If staying here is what it takes to make you believe I love you, then that's what I'll do. I don't need fame, Becca, I need you."

"Oh, Jace," she murmured, going into his arms again and hugging him. "What about your dream of a comeback? You've worked so hard."

"I wanted to prove I could make it back to the big leagues. I did that." With a gentle hand he tipped Rebecca's chin up. His fingertips stroked the curve of her cheek as he gave her a tender, earnest look. "Now I have some other things to prove—that I can be a decent husband and father."

The temptation for Rebecca to accept his decision was strong. She didn't like to think of Jace leaving, didn't like to think of all the pressure he would be under once he got to Chicago, but she didn't think she could live with herself if she kept him here.

If Jace stayed, he might always wonder if he could

have cut it had he gone back. Could he have handled the pressures of the game and the press and the specter of his past?

After all he'd gone through to change his life, he owed it to himself to prove he could handle it. Rebecca felt she owed it to him to let him find out.

She leaned up and kissed his cheek, then stood back and gazed at him as if she were memorizing the way he looked at this very moment—handsome and tough in jeans and an azure polo shirt that matched the color of his eyes. He wasn't the brash golden boy of her past. The planes and angles of his face were sharper and harder. The lines at the corners of his eyes and sensuously cut mouth had been etched there by pain and experience. The age in those eyes had been hard won.

This wasn't the Jace who had captured a young girl's heart and then carelessly broken it. This was the Jace a woman could trust her heart to and believe he would care for it and cherish it, because she loved him, because she believed in his love for her.

"I love you," she said softly. "I'm all done asking for proof, Jace. It's enough to know you'd stay if I asked you to." She offered him a gentle smile as she reached up to touch his cheek. "You go back to the big leagues and show them what Jace Cooper is made of."

"Do you mean it, Becca?"

She nodded. "I'll go with you if you need me to."

Jace thought of all the responsibilities she was willing to walk away from for him. His heart swelled with love for her. It seemed he wasn't the only one who had been growing and changing. He was tempted to take her up on her offer, but he didn't.

There were still a few things he wanted to prove to himself and to the Kings' management. If he went back, he'd go back alone, to stand on his own two feet and face up to his ghosts. He wanted to know he had

Rebecca's love and support, but she couldn't be beside him. This was something he would have to do on his own.

"No," he said, brushing her hair back from her cheek. "It's enough to know you'd go if I asked you."

Rebecca could feel it strengthen between them—the bond that had always been there deep inside. She felt it grow stronger, bridging the troubled waters of their past, pulling them to another, higher plateau, a place where love knew no insecurities, no uncertainties. And she knew in a sudden brilliant flash of insight, that this was the reward.

It had been well worth the risk.

She leaned up and kissed him, then gave him a smile that shone with all the love she felt. "Go to Chicago, Jace. I'll be waiting when you come home."

Taking her hand, he returned her smile and nodded toward the house across the alley where cats had gathered on the sagging porch to sun themselves. "Come help me pack."

Eleven

Rebecca nursed the one glass of champagne she was allowing herself in celebration, savoring the bright, sparkling taste on her tongue. Muriel's house was beautiful, she thought. The transformation it had undergone since spring had brought the old place back to life, just as Muriel's own transformation had returned her vitality and spirit.

Decked out in all its splendor for Victorian Christmas and overflowing with guests, the house glowed with life and happiness. Everyone present seemed to be glowing. And if the guests were glowing, Rebecca imagined she had to be downright radiant.

A contented, feminine smile touched her lips as she enjoyed a moment alone. For the time being, there was no one else in the hall. It was, without a doubt, the happiest day of her life, and Rebecca was glad to be sharing it with her friends, but she wanted to take a few minutes to catch her breath and gather her thoughts and feelings.

She had just left the dining room, where the long

mahogany table was laden with a dozen different dishes and Merlin moved through the crowd, dressed as a butler, serving glasses of champagne from a silver tray. Everything was going smoothly, so Rebecca took the opportunity to rest on the organ bench and gaze around at the decorations she had helped put up.

A fresh evergreen garland graced the grand staircase. There was greenery everywhere, and silky red and white bows, and bunches of dried flowers. Poinsettias of several different hues filled the bay window in the dining room, and nearly every table in the house held a bouquet of red roses accented with white baby's breath. The floral scent that filled the air was fresh and intoxicating.

In the parlor, where many of the guests were, a fresh-cut Fraser fir scratched at the nine-foot-high ceiling with its spiny spire. Many of the ornaments hanging on it had been in Muriel's family for years, some had come from France with Rebecca's maternal grandparents, and some had been painstakingly created by Justin.

Even Muriel's cats had a festive look about them—at least the ones social enough to brave the crowd. Each wore a red velvet bow around its neck.

But not everyone was decked out in Christmas finery. Christmas was still a week away. The occasion today was no less special than Christmas, Rebecca thought. In fact, it was very like Christmas in that they were celebrating life and love and wondrous new beginnings.

She smiled again and felt all sparkly inside as she lovingly ran a hand over the skirt of her satin wedding dress.

"So this is where you're hiding," Jace said softly as he slipped out of the dining room with a cheese puff in one hand.

"Hiding in plain sight." She gazed at him with what she suspected was a silly smile on her face. Her husband of three hours was incredibly handsome in a tuxedo.

Jace returned her look, his eyes shining with love. Rebecca was a vision with her midnight hair swept up in back and adorned with tiny sprigs of baby's breath. The gown she wore was very old-fashioned—puffy sleeves with tight lace cuffs, tiny seed pearls encrusting a snug bodice with a high lace collar. The rich satin fabric looked almost as creamy as her skin. The emerald he had placed on her ring finger only hours ago looked almost as exquisite as the jewel green of her eyes. The diamonds that surrounded it almost matched her sparkle.

Taking her hand in his, Jace drew her to her feet and pressed a kiss to her soft ruby lips. "You are without a doubt the most beautiful bride on the face of the earth."

Rebecca beamed and blushed, as brides are expected to do. "I think Dad might argue with you," she said. "He seems to think Muriel looks very fetching in her wedding dress too."

"And so she does," Jace conceded as he led her down the hall toward the back of the house. "I guess old Hugh knew what he was doing when he talked her into letting me room here for the summer."

Rebecca couldn't have looked more stunned if he had suddenly sprouted antlers. "He did what? My father did what?"

"Now, honey, don't get upset—"

"I'm not upset," she said, raising her hands. "I am not upset."

"You're repeating yourself," Jace pointed out, taking the champagne glass from her hand before she could spill it. He set it and his cheese puff on a table. As

Rebecca stopped in her tracks and leveled a scowl at him, he decided to spill the beans fast and get it over with. "He was the 'friend' who made my arrangements for a place to stay. I guess he figured it would be good for everyone concerned. You and I could see each other, and I could talk Muriel into getting out more, and—"

"That sneaky old fox!" she said, laughing, delighted.

"It *did* work out for everybody."

Jace pulled her into the small sitting room that had been part of his apartment. Rebecca found herself in his arms, all but purring with happiness. "I'll say," she said. "Dad ends up with Muriel. You and Dad go into business together. We end up with each other."

"I like that last part best," Jace said, sneaking a kiss. He nibbled at the teardrop pearl that hung from her left earlobe. "I love you, Mrs. Cooper."

She answered him with a sigh and a hug.

"No regrets about leaving baseball?" Rebecca asked as they snuggled together on the burgundy fainting couch.

He shook his head. "No. I made my comeback, went out on top, proved everything I needed to prove. I am very ready to settle down with my lovely bride and wonderful son and go into the robot-building business."

Rebecca kissed his cheek. "I love you, Mr. Cooper."

It seemed far too simple a thing to say for the way she felt about him. He was her best friend and her lover and her soul mate. And she was so proud of him, of the way he had exorcised his past, of the way he had fought back from his injury.

Jace was thinking of that final chapter of his career as well. He had gone back to Chicago and silenced his critics with solid playing and an attitude that proved to everyone he was a stronger, better man than the Jace Cooper they remembered. It hadn't been easy. In fact, it had probably been one of the more difficult things he'd ever had to go through in his life. But the one thing that had helped him through it was knowing he had the love and support of the woman now sitting beside him.

The day before the Kings had gone into the World Series, Jace had announced he would retire at the end of it whether his team won or lost. The Kings had lost in a seventh-game heartbreaker, but Jace had hung up his spikes and walked away happy and satisfied.

"We should go back to the party," Rebecca said with just a trace of regret in her voice. "Our guests will miss us."

"They can wait another minute or two. When I left the dining room, Turk and Mr. Peppy were getting into a rather interesting conversation with some of your dad's pals from Notre Dame. That should keep everyone distracted for a little while," Jace said with mischief dancing in his eyes. Sitting ahead, he reached into the inside breast pocket of his jacket. He handed Rebecca a small ivory envelope. "I brought you in here to give you your wedding present."

"Oh," she said in mock disappointment, her mouth settling into a sultry pout. "I thought you snuck me in here for hanky-panky."

Jace waggled his dark eyebrows at her. "You'll get all the hanky-panky you can handle tonight."

"Promises, promises," she said teasing.

She turned the envelope over and around, examining it and prolonging the anticipation. Shooting Jace a smile, she said, "At least it's not mechanical."

"No way," he said with a chuckle. "I have no desire to be electrocuted by my bride on my wedding night."

Making a face at him, she slowly opened the envelope and extracted a snapshot. It was the same snapshot he had sent to her office the day the Kings had called him back to Chicago, the photograph of their special place in the meadow by the stream.

Jace offered no explanation when she turned to him with a curious look. He leaned back and relaxed, the light of reminiscence glowing soft in his dark eyes. "Do you remember the time we walked over that hill and saw that big farmhouse there?"

She smiled fondly. "Yeah, it was yellow with blue shutters and a big porch—"

"—and oak trees in the yard. And you wondered if it didn't have a big sunny breakfast room and—"

"—polished wood floors."

Jace reached out with one finger and traced the slope of her nose. "It does."

It wasn't necessary for him to say any more than that. Rebecca knew without having to ask. Jace was giving her their meadow, the special place where they had made so many wonderful memories. It would be within walking distance of their home.

"I would have given you the deed," Jace said, "but the bank wants to hang on to that for the next thirty years or so."

"It's the thought that counts," she said, hugging him.

"It's my bonus money from the playoffs that counts," he corrected her with a grin.

"You know, I think I love baseball almost as much as I love you," she said.

Leaning back, Rebecca settled herself against his side, drawing her feet up to tuck them under her on the couch. Jace draped an arm around her and kissed her. It was a lazy kiss, one that said they had all the time in the world to please each other.

"Hey, you guys," Justin said trooping into the room. "Whatcha doing in here?"

"Smoochin'," Jace said with a grin. "Want some?"

The boy giggled as he stopped at Jace's knee. He was adorable in his miniature tux with his little bow tie askew. Rebecca had combed his black hair before the double wedding ceremony. Now one stubborn sprig had sprung free at the crown of his head. He had a smear of pink frosting from the wedding cake on his chin.

He looked up at Jace, as excited as he would be on Christmas Day, and said, "Hi, Dad!"

Everything in Jace turned warm and soft. He lifted Justin up onto his lap and hugged him. "Hi, son."

Justin settled in, snug and content. He looked up at Rebecca and said, "Now that I have a mom *and* a dad, can I get a baby brother for Christmas?"

Rebecca blushed prettily, a grin tugging at her lips. "Ask your father, sweetheart."

Jace gave her an incredulous look, then swallowed hard as he met Justin's innocent, expectant gaze. "Umm . . . ah . . ." His mind scrambled for an appropriate remark. ". . . We'll see."

It sounded more like a question than an answer. Rebecca pressed a fist to her mouth to hold back her giggles as Jace instructed Justin to go check on Merlin.

"Do you think he'll settle for a puppy?" Jace asked weakly.

"Probably."

He turned and smiled warmly at his bride. "Maybe next year we can give him a baby brother."

Rebecca fixed her gaze on her lap as she shook her head. "I don't think so."

Jace tried to ignore the pang near his heart. He was pushing her again. He had to learn to give her some room. He reached out a tentative hand to touch her shining raven's-wing hair. "I—I'm sorry, honey. If you want to wait awhile—"

"No," Rebecca said softly, nibbling at her lush lower lip. "It's not that I *want* to wait. It's that I don't think I *can* wait."

Confused, Jace stared at her a moment before uttering the classic male line. "Huh?"

With a look that held all the mystery and wisdom of women through the ages, Rebecca took his hand and drew it to the soft, shimmering fabric that fell across her stomach. "I'd say this little one isn't going to wait much longer than August."

Jace's gaze was fixed on Rebecca's elegant, long-fingered hand lying over his bigger masculine hand. Beneath his palm was the satin softness of her gown and a tiny life that had been planted there in an act of love.

It wasn't difficult to pinpoint when. Rebecca had come to Chicago to spend a few days with him between the league championship and the World Series—before he had announced his retirement, before she had gotten solid proof he would be coming home to her.

This child that was growing inside her was the ultimate symbol of her trust in him, of her love for him.

When he raised his head, there were tears in his eyes.

"I am so lucky. I thought I had it all. I thought the magic would never end, and I lived accordingly." He shook his head in wonder at both his ignorance and his newfound knowledge. "I know I never had anything worthwhile until now, until you. Thank you for believing in me, Becca."

"I love you," she whispered, and Jace smiled because there was no regret in her words, no anguish, no doubt. Only joy.

"I love you," he murmured, pulling her into his arms and holding her tight, warm, and safe as snow fell softly outside the window.

THE EDITOR'S CORNER

Get ready for a month chockfull of adventure and romance! In October our LOVESWEPT heroes are a bold and dashing group, and you'll envy the heroines who win their hearts.

Starting off the month, we have **HOT TOUCH,** LOVE-SWEPT #354. Deborah Smith brings to life a dreamy hero in rugged vet Paul Belue. When Caroline Fitz-simmons arrives at Paul's bayou mansion to train his pet wolf for a movie, she wishes she could tame the male of her species the way she works her magic with animals. The elegant and mysterious Caroline fasci-nates Paul and makes him burn for her caresses, and when he whispers "Chere" in his Cajun drawl, he melts her resistance. A unique and utterly sensual romance, **HOT TOUCH** sizzles!

Your enthusiastic response to Gail Douglas's work has thrilled us all and has set Gail's creative juices flowing. Her next offering is a quartet of books called *The Dreamweavers*. Hop onboard for your first ro-mantic journey with Morgan Sinclair in LOVESWEPT #355, **SWASHBUCKLING LADY.** Morgan and her three sisters run The Dreamweavers, an innovative travel company. And you'll be along for the ride to places exotic as each falls in love with the man of her dreams.

When hero Cole Jameson spots alluring pirate queen Morgan, he thinks he's waltzed into an old Errol Flynn movie! But Morgan enjoys her role as Captain of a restored brigantine, and she plays it brilliantly for the tourists of Key West. In Morgan, Cole finds a woman who's totally guileless, totally without pretense—and he doesn't know how to react to her honesty, espe-cially since he can't disclose his own reasons for being in Key West. Intrigued and infuriated by Cole's elusive nature, Morgan thinks she's sailing in unchar-

(continued)

tered waters. We guarantee you'll love these two charming characters—or we'll walk the plank!

One of our favorite writing teams, Adrienne Staff and Sally Goldenbaum return with **THE GREAT AMERICAN BACHELOR,** LOVESWEPT #356. Imagine you're on the worst blind date of your life . . . and then you're spirited away on a luxury yacht by a handsome hunk known in the tabloids as the Great American Bachelor! Cathy Stevenson is saved—literally—by Michael Winters when he pulls her from the ocean,.and her nightmare turns into a romantic dream. Talk about envying a heroine! You'll definitely want to trade places with Cathy in this story of a modern day Robinson Crusoe and his lady love!

Peggy Webb will take you soaring beyond the stars with **HIGHER THAN EAGLES,** LOVESWEPT #357. From the first line you'll be drawn into this powerfully evocative romance.

A widow with a young son, Rachel Windham curses the fates who've brought the irresistible pilot Jacob Donovan back from his dangerous job of fighting oil rig fires. Jacob stalks her relentlessly, demanding she explain why she'd turned her back on him and fled into marriage to another man, and Rachel can't escape—not from the mistakes of the past, nor the yearning his mere presence stirs in her. Peggy does a superb job in leading Rachel and Jacob full circle through their hurts and disappointments to meet their destiny in each other's arms.

Next in our LOVESWEPT lineup is #358, **FAMILIAR WORDS** by Mary Kay McComas. Mary Kay creates vividly real characters in this sensitive love story between two single parents.

Beth Simms is mortified when her little boy, Scotty, calls ruggedly handsome Jack Reardan "daddy" during the middle of Sunday church services. She knows that every male Scotty sees is "daddy," but

(continued)

there's something different about this man whose wicked teasing makes her blush. Jack bulldozes Beth's defenses and forges a path straight to her heart. You won't want to miss this lively tale, it's peppered with humor and emotion as only Mary Kay can mix them!

Barbara Boswell finishes this dazzling month with **ONE STEP FROM PARADISE,** LOVESWEPT #359. Police officer Lianna Novak is furious when she's transferred to Burglary, but desire overwhelms her fury when she meets Detective Michael Kirvaly. Urged on by wild, dangerous feelings for Michael, Lianna risks everything by falling in love with her new partner. Michael's undeniable attraction to Lianna isn't standard operating procedure, but the minute the sultry firecracker with the sparkling eyes approached his desk, he knew he'd never let her go—even if he had to handcuff her to him and throw away the key. Barbara will really capture your heart with this delightful romance.

We're excited and curious to know what you think of our new look, so do write and tell us. We hope you enjoy it!

Best wishes from the entire LOVESWEPT staff,

Sincerely,

Carolyn Nichols

Carolyn Nichols
Editor
LOVESWEPT
Bantam Books
666 Fifth Avenue
New York, NY 10103

60 Minutes to a Better, More Beautiful You!

Now it's easier than ever to awaken your sensuality, stay slim forever—even make yourself irresistible. With Bantam's bestselling subliminal audio tapes, you're only 60 minutes away from a better, more beautiful you!

__ 45004-2	**Slim Forever**	$8.95
__ 45112-X	**Awaken Your Sensuality**	$7.95
__ 45081-6	**You're Irresistible**	$7.95
__ 45035-2	**Stop Smoking Forever**	$8.95
__ 45130-8	**Develop Your Intuition**	$7.95
__ 45022-0	**Positively Change Your Life**	$8.95
__ 45154-5	**Get What You Want**	$7.95
__ 45041-7	**Stress Free Forever**	$7.95
__ 45106-5	**Get a Good Night's Sleep**	$7.95
__ 45094-8	**Improve Your Concentration**	$7.95
__ 45172-3	**Develop A Perfect Memory**	$8.95

NEW!
Handsome Book Covers Specially Designed To Fit Loveswept Books

Our new French Calf Vinyl book covers come in a set of three great colors— royal blue, scarlet red and kachina green.

Each 7" × 9½" book cover has two deep vertical pockets, a handy sewn-in bookmark, and is soil and scratch resistant.

To order your set, use the form below.

Special Offer
Buy a Bantam Book
for only 50¢.

Now you can have Bantam's catalog filled with hundreds of titles plus take advantage of our unique and exciting bonus book offer. A special offer which gives you the opportunity to purchase a Bantam book for only 50¢. Here's how!

By ordering any five books at the regular price per order, you can also choose any other single book listed (up to a $5.95 value) for just 50¢. Some restrictions do apply, but for further details why not send for Bantam's catalog of titles today!

Just send us your name and address and we will send you a catalog!